Tok Dalang and Stories of Other Malaysians

Tok Dalang and Stories of Other Malaysians

Ghulam-Sarwar Yousof

PARTRIDGE
A Penguin Random House Company

To order additional copies of this book, contact
Toll Free 800 101 2657 (Singapore)
Toll Free 1 800 81 7340 (Malaysia)
orders.singapore@partridgepublishing.com

www.partridgepublishing.com/singapore

Contents

PREFACE

Tok Dalang and Stories of Other Malaysians is a collection of short fiction written over several years. The stories deal with a range of characters and issues that in some ways are unique in Malaysian fiction. Traditionally Malaysian writers, depending upon their own respective racial and cultural backgrounds, have remained squarely within the "comfort zone" of their own communities, so that most stories in English as well as in other languages of the country feature the majority Malay, Chinese and Tamil Hindu communities.

In the present collection, while Malay characters still make their appearances in "Tok Dalang", "Mak Yong Dancer", "Birthday", "The Old Dictator" and "Datuk Hang Tuah", the focus has shifted to some extent into traditional culture, something rare in Malaysian writing. Additionally, lives of members of the minority communities in the country, including Tamil Muslims ("Lottery Ticket"), Sikhs ("Sujjan Singh"), Indonesians ("Dewi Ratna Sari") as well as Pakistanis ("Meditations upon a Charpoy") have been examined for the first time in Malaysian writing.

In some ways then, it is hoped that the stories in this collection will bring a new feel, as well as fresh and perhaps unique experiences for the reader of Malaysian short fiction through such characters as well as the incidents and issues which have served to shape the lives of the characters. Part of this effort has been made possible by my own personal background as someone from the north Indian or Pakistani cultural area, as well as interest as researcher in the immensely interesting South and Southeast Asian traditions of theatre.

Several of these stories were published before in my own collection entitled *Mirror of a Hundred Hues: A Miscellany* (2001).

Ghulam-Sarwar Yousof
2014

TOK DALANG

The *wayang* was in progress. The shadow play performed in Kampung Molek on many a clear, breezy night such as this from hundreds, perhaps thousands of years was in progress, the shadows prancing on the screen, colourful shades of gods and demigods, demons and humans in legendary encounters derived from the *Hikayat Seri Rama*. It was the life and blood of the villagers: simple, field-weary rustics now milling about the rickety wooden and attap *panggung* as they had for generations, waxing by turns excited or depressed as the fortunes of their green-faced divine hero, Seri Rama, his brother Laksamana, and Seri Rama's illustrious simian son changed.

Seri Rama, Laksamana and Hanuman were on their way with their colourful host of monkeys to rescue devoted Siti Dewi, Seri Rama's wife and now beautiful captive of the demon Rawana, ten-headed ruler of Langkapuri.

The other figures awaited their turn, standing in rows on the banana trunk to Tok Dalang's right or left, depending on which camp they belonged to.

The villagers recognized each and every one of the ancient characters moving across the illuminated muslin screen which, to some, the more philosophically inclined, symbolised the world, *dinding dunia*. The puppets were, like them, creatures of flesh and blood, sharing with them every human passion and Tok Dalang, he provided them with movement, with voice, with breath; indeed he gave them life. The wayang was thus a symbol of the creation and destruction of the mighty universe, for wasn't Tok Dalang indeed like God, Creator *par excellence?* No matter how much some of the more orthodox amongst them trembled away from such an association it seemed, all the same, not entirely without logic.

The wayang was in progress. It had been this way since the ancient days of Nabi Adam, regarded by some as the ancestor of all puppeteers. Tonight it was no different; Tok Dalang drew before him the all-important *pohon peringin,* world-tree, symbol of Maha Meru, link between earth and sky. Highly charged with emotion, he placed it on the banana trunk, the surface of the earth, its flickering, colourful image crisp upon the muslin. The lamp showed clearly the beads of glassy sweat on Tok Dalang's forehead and face. Slowly they trickled down his neck.

Gradually, the world-mountain began to vibrate, come alive with mysterious energy, to dance from side to side. It was the Dalang Shiva Nataraja himself, now growing faint, now clear as by turn it receded from the screen or approached it; faint and clear as Tok Dalang ritually swayed the lamp, the sun engulfing the entire universe in its brilliance. Thus, pulsating with energy, the world-mountain at last disappeared from the screen. Chaos had obtained shape and form. The mystical *mantra* of creation, the mighty voice of the Creator had been sounded, its resonance vibrating to every nook of the nascent universe, now it was time for the performance to begin.

On either side of the pohon, Tok Dalang arranged the pair of Dewa Panah, minor gods with arrows, the male principle and the female; or, according to another view, the one symbolising the negative principle, the other the positive. For wasn't the wayang after all, a symbolic clash between these two eternal principles?

Traditionally, the wayang went on for hours, often even throughout the night until the red dawn began to make itself manifest on the screen-covered eastern front of the panggung. Thus, it had been during the past few nights, the colourful heroes coming alive before hundreds of excited *kampung* eyes. Now it was the turn of Seri Rama, now that of Rawana. And now, it was the turn of Pak Dogol.

Ah yes, Pak Dogol, earthy wayang clown, brother to Vidushaka and Semar; ugly misshapen and yet incontestably divine. The amorphous figure was everybody's favourite. The audience roared with unbridled laughter at his very appearance, for who did not know Pak Dogol, god and clown, Dewa Sang Yang Tunggal descended from the sky, the object of devout reverence and mirth? He was in everybody's soul. They loved him as they loved Wak Long, created by Pak Dogol out of his own body-dirt to keep him company. Ancient wayang lore had it that Pak Dogol and Wak Long together served first Rawana and then, after the demon's defeat, the handsome Seri Rama, just and victorious ruler of Siusia Mendarapura.

There was unrestrained laughter, reaching far into the moonlit kampung among the ghostly coconut palms, and mingling even with the cool mountain breeze that fanned the panggung; laughter occasionally punctuated by an excited scream as Tok Dalang signalled the musicians or emphasized a point one of his characters was making; laughter punctuated by the vibrant, deep-voiced *gong ibu*.

Thus, the wayang continued, played by the Tok Dalang, the most famous in Kampung Molek and for miles around, played as he had learnt it from his illustrious master, Dalang Pak Su Jusoh, played in the same unmistakable manner Tok Dalang had used during the past twenty years: the drama of gods and demons, the drama in which the mysterious, androgynous Pak Dogol was always present—bald, misshapen, with bulging belly, a large and out of proportion navel, sagging breasts, his buttocks tilted upwards and his large, hooked nose.

In the night, the thump-thumping of the clamorous orchestra sounded way beyond the breezy valley in which Kampung Molek nestled. It was carried to the foothills of Gunung Berahi whence it returned, echoing sharply. In particular, the shrill, vital shriek of the *serunai* stood out, bisecting the night, punctuated by the vibrant deep-voiced *gong ibu.*

Tok Dalang's hands moved agilely, the puppets responding to every subtle shift. Looking at the shirtless, *sarung*-clad Tok Dalang, one could not imagine such energy issuing out of his system, out of that one single, slim built person: all the voices, loud and soft, pleading and threatening, masculine and feminine; all the movements, violent and subtle. It was indeed a superhuman task. He was a live-wire, Tok Dalang, moving continuously with the intense energy that charged his frail system as it filled also the puppets and the living instruments. One could understand his fame; appreciate the fact that he had travelled far and wide enthralling thousands beyond the shores of his native Malaysia.

One often hears of the magic of the wayang, of its ability to intoxicate. One has to watch someone like Tok Dalang to appreciate its magic. It is said that to assist him, many a performer retains his own attendant spirit, using powerful magic formulae known only to him. It is said too, that one possessed by a particularly powerful spirit gathers from that invisible beings some of its superhuman strength, becoming from time to time uncontrollable. Tonight, as he animated the cow-skin figures, Tok Dalang seemed to be possessed by some such superior, inexplicable force: a force which carried him to heights of ecstasy. Quite often, he was oblivious of all else, like a good actor altogether immersed in his character.

At other times, as he moved the figures effortlessly, without any specific thought, his mind wandered...

He remembered the many locations at which he had performed since the days when, as a young apprentice puppeteer, he first learnt to play the *Dalang Muda* episode; the many wayang competitions he had won in festivals held regularly in his part of the country but now, for the past six years, altogether abandoned. Those were the days of the wayang; he couldn't help but reflect when dozens of puppeteers like him would display their skills, each attempting to outshine the other in the magical cosmic drama.

Yes, the wayang was imbued with magic, a subtle, indefinable kind of magic, and no one felt it more strongly tonight than Tok Dalang. He remembered the many gifts he had received, the prizes and trophies he had won, the awards and decorations. He was the supreme Dalang, the Dalang of all puppeteers. At this unconscious thought, a cold shudder ran through him, his skin became covered with goose-pimples.

"No, no, that was not true, not true." He quickly muttered an apology to the gods for a careless blasphemy. He was but a mere earthly being, a mortal dependant totally for inspiration and skills upon that Superior Being, the Dalang of all dalang.

His thoughts reverted to the huge audiences at the wayang festivals, to the women he had met, women who had been fascinated by his art as much as by his person, women who had been drawn irresistibly to him. Such was the power of the magical *mantera* he used. He had lost count of how many women had been drawn to him, mercilessly charmed by him, women who had without the slightest resistance surrendered themselves to him. Such was his power as dalang and bomoh. A few of the more beautiful faces passed before him on the kaleidoscope of his mind, some of the more memorable forms. He even thought he smelt a whiff of familiar perfume.

Rawana was making yet another attempt to win over Siti Dewi, the desire within him getting uncontrollable each passing instant. He watched her and her beauty got possession of him. He had been trying all manner of persuasion and flattery to which he believed all women are susceptible. But he had not succeeded. He had tried coercion and threats, but she remained coldly inviolate. His suffering was immense. Now, for the hundredth time, he had come to her, determined to succeed. They were alone, her attendants and companions having been brusquely sent off by him. It was a cool spring night. The atmosphere was romantic enough, the fragrant flowers in his garden in full bloom, like Siti Dewi herself, beckoning to be plucked. He came to visit her, whispering that he had loved her for many a year from a distance, whispering that news had reached him of Rama's death. The path was now open for her to become the queen of his heart, the queen of the greatest ruler on earth, the queen of ancient Langkapuri.

As he watched her sitting on her couch, her long hair falling over her shoulders, touching softly the pale nape of her neck and trailing between her breasts, her lips quivering, his desire rose violent within him. But he controlled himself. He did not want to reveal himself uncouth, for uncouthness did not become a devotee of beauty. No need for violence. Persuasion. Yes, persuasion and flattery. The promise of wealth and power. Was there any woman who would not succumb to these things?

But Siti Dewi continued to resist him, naming him demon, thief, a coward to kidnap her thus, comparing him to the gentle green-faced Rama, her glorious husband, who had heroically won her at an open contest for her hand in the land of her father, defeating the world's rulers. Rawana felt ashamed, his anger intermingled with his lust, both building up powerful within him. He remembered his defeat at that marriage-competition, his ignominious defeat at the hands of Seri Rama, the skeleton of a man. He screamed a thunderous scream that shook his palace, was heard far beyond its confines. Siti Dewi's attendants and the king's soldiers came scurrying in. Once again, Rawana had failed. Once again, Siti Dewi remained unravished.

Thus Tok Dalang continued his *wayang*, Siti Dewi, beauteous wife of Seri Rama, and the women in his own life merging into a single lusty image of womanhood, sharp and clear in his mind, an image surrounded by a faint whiff of familiar perfume.

The scream of the *serunai* drew Tok Dalang out of his reverie, his face lit in a whimsical smile. The sweat streaked down his intense neck. The music continued its throb. Now with a loud yell, he brought onto the screen the white figure of Hanuman, pouncing left and right, in battle with the ferocious Inderajit. The orchestra picked up *lagu perang,* the piece to accompany battles. The battle heated up, rising to a crescendo, made uncomfortable by the glowing heat of the lamp.

Many had seen the battles thus fought on the white muslin, the many monkey generals emerging one by one. Tonight, somehow, there was something different about the battles and about the wayang. The audience felt it, the musicians sensed it, and Tok Dalang, in his heart of hearts knew that tonight's performance was special. There was immense vitality in the air. The atmosphere was electrified. The figures moved with greater vibrancy than ever before, and Tok Dalang's voice, whether he was speaking or singing, floated vehement into the hearts and souls on the other side of the screen, and way beyond the vicinity of the *panggung.*

Tok Dalang could not see his entire audience from his position on the panggung. He could, however, see a good number of persons through the gaps between the screen and the panggung-wall, through the leaves of potted croton plants. But the voices of his audience members he could hear and he could sense their excitement. His estimation was that there must be a thousand people there, young and old, male and female. None of them moved away, so captivated were they by the spirit of the wayang. True, before the mysterious ritual dance of the *pohon peringin*, he had ceremoniously opened the theatre with incantations and invocations addressed to the invisible beings. He had taken especial care that evening to include a few particularly powerful *ayat* from the *Holy Quran*. Perhaps, it was due to the efficacy of the *mantera* and the verses from the *Holy Quran* that the crowd was larger, the performance better than usual.

Tok Dalang recalled the instructions he had received from Pak Su Jusoh many years ago in the use of these particular verses. Now, he sensed the old man's wisdom. Tok Dalang had used that evening a particular strong *pemanis*, a charm of personal attraction. This pemanis had always been efficacious in drawing people to him, whether or not he was operating the wayang. Above all, the night was a brilliantly successful one due to the special favour of the invisible ever-present Ultimate Dalang. He had no doubt about this.

Many were the battles fought on the white screen illuminated by a single lamp. Many were the epic battles raging in Tok Dalang's soul. In all circumstances, close to all that transpired, stood the dark, inevitable figure of Pak Dogol.

The god-clown now appeared on the screen, in battle with a dragon, guardian of a sacred tree. The monster had succeeded in defeating both Seri Rama and his valiant younger brother, Laksamana, in furious battles several days along. Now, Pak Doggol had to intervene, for he, the omniscient Dewa Sang Yang Tunggal, knew the monster's true identity. It was a minor *dewa* from Kayangan, the Sky-country. Pak Dogol was confident that the battle would end with the dewa's inevitable defeat and retransformation. Seri Rama could thus continue his journey after eating the sacred fruit. Fate drew him towards Langkapuri, towards that final contest with Rawana for which both the hero and the demon king had been reincarnated on earth. This was the great design of the gods; Siti Dewi but a means to an end.

Tok Dalang moved the figures, expertly drawing the curves of confrontation between the dragon and Pak Dogol. Pak Dogol thrust his wooden *golok* at the dragon; the beast, in turn, opened the cavern of his wide, fiery mouth to singe Pak Dogol. The battle seemed endless, both protagonists immortal. The audience was excited as were the musicians. And Tok Dalang himself...it gave him an indescribable sense of power, power even over metaphysical forces.

And then, like a sudden flash of lightning, something happened, something strange and inexplicable. At the lifting of Pak Dogol, the old man once again preparing to enter the fray, Tok Dalang's soul shrank. There was fear in his heart. Never before in his twenty years as puppeteer had such fear manifested itself. A cold shudder left him trembling like a leaf in a black night wind. He felt the impetuous passing of an electrical current through his sinews from his right hand that held Pak Dogol through his arm into his body and thence straight into the very root of his being. It left him cold as ice. His hand became uneasy. His body began to vibrate, in rhythm with the music. The shrill voice of the *serunai* pierced the stillness of night as it pierced the soul of Tok Dalang, reaching a mile or more beyond the valley, in which the hamlet nestled, tearing the silence of night in its process. Tok Dalang's hand, manipulated now it seems by some superior external force, continued the ritual drama, human versus animal, divine versus demoniac . . . the never-ending conflict in every human soul.

Tok Dalang took a series of slow breaths to regain his composure, silently reciting several times the *auzubillah*, the formula of protection. He told himself the fear was completely unfounded. Nothing would happen. After all, he had not many evenings ago, as was the custom in the wayang world, made the necessary ritual offerings: parched rice, flowers, water, *beras kunyit*, raw thread and some money. It had all been done in the traditional manner as transmitted to him by Pak Su Jusoh, the most famous dalang of his time. Pak Su Jusoh had derived the techniques from his teacher and legendary Dalang Pak Dollah. Tok Dalang was indeed the scion of illustrious forbears.

The shadows were the reality, the puppets mere casters of shadows, the shadows that connected him, Tok Dalang and the Kampung Molek villagers to the spirit world of their ancestors, the progenitors of the Nusantara race. And there, above all, in this world of shadows and ancestors, stood Pak Dogol, Semar, Dewa Sang Yang Tunggal.

The shadows upon the screen began to blur as tears gradually misted Tok Dalang's eyes. He felt helpless; a piercing sense of coldness pervaded his senses. He stopped the wayang, the figure of Pak Dogol in his right hand; he heard the thump-thumping of the instruments, the sharp call of the hypnotizing night-piercing *serunai* punctuated by the pair of gongs, *tetawak*. Tok Dalang stopped the wayang. His companions, the musicians, unaware of what was happening, were confused. The music continued, for the musicians were afraid to stop lest the spirits took offence at any unorthodox breaking off of the music. The screen remained bare, a world without inhabitants.

Tok Dalang could vaguely sense the audience impatience. The crowd became increasingly restless as each second passed without the figures reappearing. The music sounded louder. His musicians began to question him. Did he feel unwell or need a rest? All this

Tok Dalang could not hear. His eyes were filled with tears, the lamp before him now a fuzzy orb of golden fire. He was far, far away, in some distant dimension, a layer of the universe quite alien from his own.

He could not continue. Suddenly, he placed the pohon peringin at the screen centre, piercing the banana trunk with one louder scream — the pohon peringin, world- mountain, sacred Maha Meru, mountain of the gods, link between earth and sky, vibrating for a moment, cast its shaky shadows on the white muslin. Tok Dalang's eyes were still fuzzy, his head reeling, the thumping of music growing increasingly louder in his ears, increasing in his head, louder and louder in his entire system, piercing the immeasurable silences of his soul, deeper and deeper, sharper and sharper. And then . . .

And then. . . something cracked in him. Tok Dalang was no longer himself. He stood up and began to gyrate jerkily, Pak Dogol in his hand, his head rotating. He danced lithely like the very figures he had been animating only moments before. The dance had about it something of the *main puteri* shaman dance. The musicians were stunned and fascinated at the same time. They continued playing, playing and Tok Dalang danced, his stance unmistakable. The god had arrived.

The musicians muttered inaudible supplications. Tok Dalang threw the figure of Pak Dogol onto the wooden floor. The tune changed into *lagu puteri*, while Tok Dalang danced energetically, almost violently in that unmistakable pose. It was no longer a mere wayang. It was the dance of Pak Dogol, Semar, Dewa Sang Yang Tunggal. Yes, Dewa Sang Yang Tunggal, the mightiest of gods, had arrived.

"What is happening?"

"Oi, what happened to the wayang?"

"Carry on with the wayang."

The restive crowd could not see behind the *kelir*, restricted as it was to the world of shadows. The Dalang Muda made a terse announcement. The wayang performance was over for the evening. The audience murmured in disappointment. Crowds surged onto the back of the panggung, the frail structure groaning under their weight. The Dalang Muda tried to stop them from entering but to no avail.

"There has been a *menurun*." One of the musicians said.

"Please get off the panggung. It will collapse."

There was some commotion. Most of the audience members paid no heed to the words. Those who could see into the interior through the *panggung's* narrow door saw the entranced Tok Dalang. Some were benumbed. Others muttered silent prayers. Yet, others executed the *sembah* gesture.

Once the incident had fully registered itself in their minds, the crowd began to disperse, murmuring like hundreds of bees when their hive is disturbed. Some lingered on to see what would happen next. The musicians continued to play, not for Tok Dalang, for Tok Dalang was no longer there, nor was there any more wayang. The appearance of the pohon peringin on the kelir had marked its end. They were playing for Dewa Sang Yang Tunggal who had come amongst them in person.

Soon, the whole village was humming with the news, the voices floating past the staid, ghostly coconut palms. The music continued, the serunai piercing into the depths of night.

"Call Tok Bomoh," someone suggested.

"Yes, call Pak Su Jusoh."

"Call the Tok Bomoh. Call Pak Su Jusoh. Call the Tok Bomoh. Call Pak Su Jusoh."

Several voices joined in as the message got relayed. Yes, only Pak Su Jusoh could handle the situation. He had immense *ilmu dalam*, he was an experienced bomoh. Pak Su Jusoh was soon aroused from an early but restless sleep. He came, muttering to himself. The venerable Pak Su Jusoh swore under his breath.

"*Celaka sungguh.* These people will not even let an old man have some peace. What's the meaning of all this? Has the sky fallen down? Tell me, quick. Why do you come in such unruly fashion to disturb an old man's sleep?"

In his heart of hearts, he knew that something was seriously the matter, or the crowd would not have thus ventured to disturbed the peace of night.

"What is the matter, huh?" Even while Pak Su Jusoh was mumbling his questions, excited and disjoined voices had begun telling him what had happened. There had been a menurun at Tok Dalang's wayang kulit performance. Dewa Sang Yang Tunggal had appeared. Only he, Pak Su Jusoh, could deal with Dewa Sang Yang Tunggal. Pak Su Jusoh's eyes lit up at the mention of the god. It was as if he recognised in that name an old friend.

"Are you sure it's Dewa Sang Yang Tunggal?"

"That's what they said at the panggung." He went into his hut to make his preparations.

"Quick, quick Pak Su! Please help, Pak Su!" A terrified breathless female voice now joined in. Some recognised it as belonging to Limah, Tok Dalang's wife. She had just heard the news and had come running all the way from her home.

"Ha, wait. Let me get my things together." Pak Su Jusoh did not even bother to think who it might be. It was just another voice among the night's multitude of anonymous voices. But Dewa Sang Yang Tunggal . . .

Pak Su Jusoh soon emerged, a bundle of things and a *tongkat* in his hands, a white *kepiah* on his head. He looked like Tok Maharisi himself. The crowd made their way excited before him. The serunai could be heard from a distance; the music became louder as they approached the panggung.

Pak Su Jusoh ordered everyone to remain outside, chasing off the panggung its earlier invaders. Only Limah was allowed to remain. Pak Su sat cross-legged on the mat-covered floor. He signalled the musicians to stop playing. The dancing Tok Dalang, sweat pouring in rivulets down his back, collapsed on to the floor, now suddenly weak and exhausted as if it was the music that had sustained him, providing him with the tremendous vitality he displayed only moments before. He knelt on the mat, panting heavily, his hands on the floor before him. Pak Su took a handful of rice, whispered a silent mantera into it as he held his hand to his mouth and then threw the uncooked rice violently about the panggung to chase away any malicious influence. Some of the rice was similarly sprayed upon Tok Dalang's still-quivering body. Pak Su sprinkled some drops of water on Tok Dalang's face and head, water over which he had read *ayat* from the *Holy Quran*. Tok Dalang became calm. Then Pak Su Jusoh began his rituals, beginning with the *Audhubillah* and the *Basmala,* proceeding into other lengthy recitations.

"*Nenek,* we are extremely honoured with your presence tonight," he began in tone both severe and familiar, "But why, Grandsire, have you come?"

"Oh, so you recognise me." Semar reacted, amused.

"Yes, *Nenek,* your grandchild here recognised you immediately. Tell me, Grandsire, why have you come?"

Semar answered. He had come to receive the offerings promised him several years ago when a *berjamu* wayang had been planned. The *niat* had been made, but no performance had taken place. On behalf of Tok Dalang, the confident Pak Su Jusoh apologised for the omission.

"It shall be done, *Nenek*. It shall be done without fail. This I promise you."

"When?"

"Soon, Grandsire, soon. You will receive your offerings at the proper place at the appropriate time in the customary manner.

"When?" asked Semar again.

"As soon as possible, *Nenek*. Please forgive your grandchild and the innocent Tok Dalang for this negligence, *Nenek.*"

"And what about now? Do I get anything this time?"

"Yes, Grandsire. You will receive something this time, but not very much; there is no berjamu."

"When?"

"Tomorrow morning, *Nenek*. At first light of dawn when the *murai* bird begins to sing, when the elephant turns on its side to sleep, under the shade of the mango trees in the far corner of the *kampong* we will place for your pleasure certain offerings of food."

"Alright, tomorrow morning then, and without fail."

"Yes, tomorrow morning, *Nenek,* without fail."

"Very well."

"Please have patience, Grandsire, and forgive us our error, for we humans are indeed weak, *Nenek.*"

Tok Bomoh Pak Su Jusoh signalled the musicians, who played a short piece. The old man sprinkled rice on the panggung floor, and wiped Tok Dalang's face with ritually prepared water. Tok Dalang gradually regained his consciousness, his personality. He was only vaguely aware of the divine visitation.

As promised, some offerings were placed for the god the very next morning under the trees at the edge of the kampung. Three months later, an elaborate three-night berjamu performance, replete with all paraphernalia and elaborate food offerings, took place.

That was many years ago. The little giggling girls who at that time ran about naked but for their *caping* in the kampong or constantly bent down to pick up their falling *sarungs* had all grown up. Some had even married and become mothers. Tok Bomoh Pak Su Jusoh died a long time ago, and lay buried in the cemetery at the kampung's rim. Now, there was a proper road reaching that spot. Kampung Molek had even received electricity and clean piped water flowed from the few public taps. Most of the village folk could not afford the cost of getting their own connections.

And there, in the eastern corner of the kampung, on the landing of an old, dilapidated hut, sat an ancient man, bald and grey-bearded, staring into empty space, his eyes fixed. He was chewing on betel leaves. Drops of saliva flowed down from his mouth.

Tok Dalang had already lost count. Hundreds, perhaps thousands, had come to him over the years, some to seek blessing or holy water, others to obtain cures for sundry maladies, and yet, others, a few, mostly university students, to question him regarding the wayang, regarding Semar. He had always given a simple answer: it was a mystery beyond human comprehension, the wayang. No one could understand the mystery of the wayang, the identity of Semar, unless one became part of it, became entranced by it. It was no use talking about it. One had to live through it, become a true dalang.

"Is it a sin, the wayang?" Every now and then someone had boldly ventured to ask. Tok Dalang had laughed his now rare and mysterious laugh, revealing the single betel-stained tooth in a cavernous mouth.

"You cannot understand the meaning of sin, my child. Few can, although many claim the ability to do so. The mysteries of right and wrong, like the mysteries of life and death, are beyond us. They are beyond us all."

"Like the mystery of the wayang?"

"Yes, like the mystery of the wayang?"

"Like the mystery of the dark, misshapen Semar."

"Yes, like the dark, misshapen Semar. These mysteries are known only to God."

Some thought the old man was losing his mind. Others thought he was a saint, a *wali*. Thus, his hut became a shrine for all manner of people; to some the abode of an old and insane ex-puppeteer; to others a shrine with a living *keramat* to which they were drawn again and again, both young and old, from long distances, in search of blessings or favours, for the fulfilment of a thousand mundane needs and desires: healing, the birth of a child; or merely the overwhelming urge to satisfy curiosity.

His considerable inner knowledge, *ilmu kebatinan*, had been recognised far and wide during his younger days as an active dalang. His love charms were then famous, and many a Kampung Molek parent had to keep his daughters under constant vigil for fear they would be seduced by the handsome, magical Tok Dalang. Over the years, his spiritual powers had been further enhanced. There were stories told of how he had spent days, weeks, even months on end, meditating unstintingly in a cave on Gunung Berahi without even eating a morsel. Indeed, Allah had blessed him with superior learning. So some thought. On the other hand, some had named him Tok Dalang Gila, the mad puppeteer. To some, he was a pious Haji, a good Muslim, and to others, who knew his dalang days, he was known as an unrepentant devotee of Semar, so that among his less often expressed nicknames were Tok Dalang Semar or Tok Dalang Dogol. Some claimed to discern in his ancient body the form of the ugly, misshapen Semar. Others would swear his powers enabled him to levitate, that he was seen at one place now and at another the next instance, or even simultaneously at more than one place.

And so, when he died, many could not believe such an event possible. They had begun to regard his as a *wali,* a god incarnate; they had thought that one day he would altogether disappear. Physical death was not for the likes of him.

His death, by all accounts, was a peaceful one, although some had expected it to be otherwise. They had heard of Semar devotees who had a difficult time dying, had believed that, like them, Tok Dalang too would suffer before breathing his last unless he renounced the god.

After an elaborate funeral attended by a good number of Kampung Molek villagers and by many others who came from far and near, Tok Dalang was buried according to his desire, in a simple grave in the village cemetery at the rim of the kampung.

That was many years ago. The little giggling girls who at that time ran about naked in the kampung have all grown up. The village has become a little township, with a market of its own. Tok Dalang's grave is, to this day, visited by many who treat it as *keramat.* Some claim to have heard on occasional nights the sounding of faint gongs or the sad strains of a *serunai.* One wandering in its vicinity can see, on almost any day, numerous flowers strewn over it, smell a faint whiff of familiar perfume, as if the surrounding gardens and trees have themselves conspired to make Tok Dalang immortal.

LOTTERY TICKET

As Aboo Bakar Maraicar said his prayers that rainy Friday afternoon, he found it more difficult than usual to concentrate. The voice of the *imam* seemed so distant and his words had about them only a vague ring of familiarity. Not that Aboo Bakar was a scholar or even moderately educated in religious matters. He was just an ordinary Muslim, neither pious nor yet completely ignorant of Islamic tenets. He was familiar with some of the Hadith and the stories of the prophets; he knew a few verses from the Holy Quran but, even he had to admit to himself, not quite enough to get him through prayers. Thus his attempts to pray were not entirely successful.

Like most Muslims he ritually omitted the five obligatory prayers every day, but he made sure he went to the Kapitan Keling mosque on Fridays for the Jumaat communal prayers and for the two Eid prayers every year. Somehow that had been the pattern of his religious life since he first started going to the mosque with his now deceased father, Abdul Kadir Maraicar more than thirty-five years ago in his little village outside Nagapattinam. Always, the concentration was not complete. He did not speak or understand Arabic, and so the prayers and the Quranic verses were no more than pleasant sounding words with an aura of the sacred. Some, of course, like the *Kalimah Shahadat* and other constantly repeated phrases including *Astaghfirullah* and *Inshaallah* he had, even as a child, come to understand and to take seriously. But the longer *doa* and passages from the Holy Quran meant very little to him, their sonority apart, for even he, in his ignorance, had to admit that the language had a strange beauty about it, particularly as recited by the *imam* in the Kapitan Keling mosque, the well-known Hafiz Mansoor Avargal.

For him it had been the fashion or rather the habit to attend these gatherings for they were *sunnat* and because his companion salesmen and coworkers from the neighbouring shops did so. He sometimes wondered, though, where all this want of concentration and even more, his near-complete lack of understanding of ritual texts was to lead him, especially when it came to *Hari Qiamat*, the Day of Resurrection and Judgment, when he would come face to face with his Maker, Allah. He must try to become more familiar with the prayers both in their content and in their method of performance, he once again resolved, realizing too, suddenly that his ankles hurt with his whole weight placed on them for some time now, as he listened to the *khutbah*. He shifted his weight to the other foot, establishing himself comfortably, removing the tightness in his white *sarung*. He wished the sermon would end. It seemed interminable.

While for Aboo Bakar Maraicar concentration during prayers had always been a problem—his mind tended to move from one thought to another, today it was proving even more difficult than usual. This was because he had only that morning looked into the *Tamil Nesan* and made the pleasant discovery that he had won a lottery. His Social Welfare lottery ticket entitled him to a sum of $25,000.00. Feeling elated since the discovery, he wondered how much greater, how much more intense, the excitement would have been if he had won the first prize of $450,000.00. When he reflected upon this figure his mind reeled. He could not even imagine such a big sum of money.

He was certain that if he ever won first prize he would go insane or die from the shock of it. He had heard stories derived from friends or occasionally published in newspapers in which winners of such huge sums of money had died out of shock or completely uncontrollable pleasure.

Others had to go into hiding or even go overseas for fear they would become victims of robbers and murderers intent upon getting their hands upon the money.

So he was glad that his prize was neither the first, nor the second nor the third but just one of the consolation prizes. Reverently, closing his eyes for a moment, he thanked Allah for the gift, the first he had ever received though the two or three Social Welfare lottery tickets that he had made it a point to buy every month without fail. With a *Bismillah* he put his right hand into his pocket, took out the ticket for examination, and placed it back quickly, realizing that he was being observed by several pairs of curios eyes. He smiled, and nodded at one or two persons seated near him. Yes, he was unmistakably a winner.

Hafiz Mansoor's voice rolled on sonorously. Today's sermon was on avarice, and the need for good Muslims to avoid greed, for it led to behaviour contrary to Islamic teachings.

He wondered if the acquisition of the lottery money could be equated with avarice; if his act of buying lottery tickets every month could be considered an act of greed. Hope and expectation there certainly were, but greed? He was not too sure.

A part of the money, he decided, would be sent to India, to assist his family. The regular remittances out of his salary of $350.00 were small. He saved every cent he could on food and clothes-just an occasional new *sarung* or a shirt, and that too usually at the time of *Hari Raya*. He paid a mere $40.00 a month for a place to lay his mat each night in a room with five others, just a few shop-houses

away from where he worked. He never allowed himself any luxuries:
a couple of Tamil or Hindustani films every month at the Royal or
Paramount theatres, usually on Sundays, and his *beedi*. His family
needed the rest of his earnings; and so every two or three months he
sent them whatever he managed to save, keeping aside a little for his
return ticket to India and some shopping at the end of his present
tour of work in Penang. He had already completed slightly more
than two years. Another eighteen months to two years at the most
and he would leave, sailing on the S.S. Chidambaram or perhaps
taking a flight, if he could manage that. Sometimes a good annual
profit by his firm, Ghulam Mustapha & Sons, meant a generous
gift from his employer. He had been fortunate enough in the past
to receive a big enough bonus to buy his air ticket. Yet, he had to be
prepared for the worst.

He preferred to sail, for that way he could carry much more
luggage, besides the usual gifts, including some jewellery for his
family members. Typically his additional luggage, like that carried
by many of his companions who, like him, returned to Tamil Nadu
for family visits once in every two or three years, would include
a large tin of biscuits, several tins of Milo or Ovaltine, Japanese
slippers, some clothing, a transistor radio or two, an electric iron,
watches, ballpoint pens and dark glasses, sometimes a shirt or two,
came in handy as gifts for the Customs officers at Madras. It was
an investment, for by giving these gifts he could get away without
paying any duty, or by paying just a small amount. Dark glasses
usually served this purpose pretty well. Once in Madras he could
make some profit selling items he did not need.

Yes, any additional money he sent would be of help to his
family, and now, through the lottery ticket, Allah had given him
the opportunity to make some preparations for any unexpected
situation that may rise. His children were growing up, and his two

daughters Aminah and Ayesha, named after wives of the Prophet Muhammad, peace and blessings be upon him, would have to be married off in the coming years. He had to provide for their sarees, jewellery and the wedding feast. There was also the dowry to be paid. These matters would be settled when he next went to India, he decided. His son, Pakeer Mohamed, was not doing well in school and would probably one day join him in Penang, or start a small business in Nagapattinam. Aboo Bakar was thankful that with the winning of the lottery he would be better able to settle at least some of his family matters. God has indeed been kind and merciful to him, *Alhamdulillah.*

Hafiz Mansoor was still going on about the dangers and pitfalls of greed, quoting profusely from the holy *Quran* and the *Hadith* to substantiate his points, translating these passages into Bahasa Malaysia and even, occasionally, into Tamil for the likes of our hero. Aboo Bakar Maraicar did not realize until now that there was so much in the Holy Quran and in the Prophet's sayings about greed and avarice. He had believed that the Holy Quran contained mainly injunctions about prayers, fasting and the pilgrimage to Mecca besides the stories about the series of prophets from Nabi Adam to Nabi Muhammad. What a pity, he thought that he could neither read nor understand the Arabic of the Holy Quran. The only religious instruction he managed to obtain was on Fridays during these *khutbah.*

He closed his eyes, trying to listen intently, to concentrate. This exercise worked for only a minute or two. He found, as usual, that his mind kept wandering. Sometimes, when hungry, he imagined what awaited him at lunch after prayers. Friday's lunch at Jabarullah's dingy restaurant at the corner of Market Street and Queen Street was always special. There would be chicken curry and vegetables to go with *nasi minyak,* or if he was lucky, it may even be *nasi beriani.*

Friday's lunch made up for all the unpalatable food during the remaining days of the week.

True, there were all sorts of tempting dishes available, but the likes of him could not afford them. He and others like him--salesmen, port workers, and coolies--invariably made special arrangements with the *Mamak* restaurants in the Little India area. For a fixed monthly payment they would get a meal at lunch time and again at dinner time. There was no limit on the rice but the curry and meat dishes were rationed. What more, the curry was always watered down and *dalcha* made its appearance much too often. But Aboo Bakar knew that, considering that the amount he and his companions paid was only $100.00 per month, they could not expect much better food. Well, at least today was Friday. Overall, he decided, he had no reason to complain.

Once in a while he got invited to his employer's house for a meal, a privilege not enjoyed by many of his friends who served other masters, and occasionally there were weddings when the food turned out to be quite good, even superb. Yes, he could not afford luxuries, but he had no real reason to complain either, especially now that he had received the unexpected bonus.

Aboo Bakar Maraicar decided that after a portion of his windfall had been sent off to India by the usual black market arrangement, he would place the rest in a savings account at a local bank until it was time for him to return to Nagapattinam. This money he would invest upon reaching India--perhaps he could buy some land in his village and lease it out, or he could buy a house or two and become a landlord . . . there were numerous possibilities. To each he gave a minute or two of his time while his mind raced about in other directions imagining the most lucrative manner in which his money could be utilized . . . he could start a restaurant and then there would be no need to return to Malaysia to work as a salesman; he could become a *mudalali* with his own textiles business or a partnership with someone in Nagapattinam. He could sense the excitement building up inside him as these schemes raced through his head. The sermon ended, and the *imam* now descended from the pulpit to take his place at the head of the congregation. The words of the *azan* were recited again. The worshippers stood up to get into long straight rows, pushing against each other in preparation for the prayers. Silence descended upon the congregation.

Allahu Akbar. He raised his hands and placed them on his belly, the right over the left, his shoulders touching those of the young Malay in red *baju Melayu* on his left and the older, bearded and heavily perfumed Mamak like him on his right. The mosque was crowded, as it usually was during Friday prayers.

Hafiz Masoor's voice was mesmerizing as he read the Surah al-Fatihah and a much longer passage from the Holy Quran, a section Aboo Bakar was not familiar with. Aboo Bakar listened, but he could not get his mind off his lottery ticket. He was tempted to put his hand in his pocket to make sure the ticket was safely in place, but resisted the temptation, tried to draw his mind back to the prayer. *Allahu Akbar.* He prostrated himself for the *ruku. Allahu Akbar.* He stoop up straight again. Then, with another *Allahu Akbar,* he went down for the *sujud* with the rest of the congregation.

After what seemed like an eternity the prayers came to an end with a long final supplication. Aboo Bakar shook hands with his immediate neighbours. The rush out of the mosque began, and the mosque itself now noisy with the sounds of greetings and conversation. Aboo Bakar was still sitting on the floor. He became conscious that people were pushing him, walking past him. It was time for lunch. He became aware of his sore ankle, and stood up, limping for a moment to gain his balance. He shook hands with several of those he recognized in the crowd, but then waited for the rush at the Pitt Street exit to thin out before leaving. Limping slowly towards the *mihrab* he waited his turn to shake hands with Hafiz Mansoor Avargal. This was not his usual practice, but this particular Friday he made it a point to greet the *imam*. It was, after all, no ordinary Friday, and who knows whose blessings had been responsible for his good fortune?

Still inwardly jubilant he left the mosque, crossing Pitt Street and passing the row of jewellery shops. The *nasi minyak* or *nasi beriani* awaited him in Jabbarullah's restaurant. He looked forward to a good meal. It was almost two o'clock, well past his non-Friday lunch time when there were no *Jumaat* prayers to attend. Today he had to eat fast for he had an important mission to complete.

Earlier in the day he had decided that after prayers and lunch he would make inquiries about the manner in which his ticket could be converted into cash. This was, for him, an entirely new situation. He considered it important at this point to keep his good fortune a secret even from his friends and companions. During lunch he remained silent, relishing both the chicken *beriani* and the thought of better things awaiting him in the near future.

"Aboo Bakar *Annai,* what's the problem? You are so quiet today, brother." It was the voice of his one of his regular eating companions, Shahul Hameed. Shahul Hameed was a salesman like Aboo Bakar Maraicar, only much younger. There was a gap of more than twenty years between the two.

"Oh, Shahul Hameed, nothing. Nothing is the matter."

"You're so quiet. Hope everything is alright. Any news from the family in India?"

"Yes, they're all fine. I received a letter from the village only three days ago. And how are things with you?"

"Nothing special. You know there's not much excitement in the life of a salesman. Its work and work and work six days a week and then the Sunday off . . . a Sunday you don't know what to do with. I have not been to the cinema for the past month. Just work and then a walk to the Esplanade to ogle at the passing women; dinner and back to the room. That's life for us, and soon, before we realize it, we will be dead. At least I hope I die in the village in India and not in this alien land, so that the family can perform the last rites. This poor, stinking life; and yet people in Tamil Nadu believe we are minting money here. There's no end to their increasing demands."

"But you don't have to worry. You're not even married; so you don't have a family to support back home."

"Well, yes, But *Annai,* I have my old parents to think about, and a pair of younger sisters to marry off. So something has to be sent home every now and then, you know."

"Don't you ever plan to get married yourself, here or back home?"

"No, I haven't even thought about it, although my parents have been hinting in their letters that they may have someone in mind for me in India, a distant cousin. But what's the point? If I do get married, my wife will have to stay in India while I live here in Penang, going back once in every two or three years. What kind of a life would that be? Well I don't have to tell you. You know much better about these things than I do."

"Yes." Aboo Bakar knew a great deal of the struggles, the hardships involved, he had been living in that manner--going between Penang and Nagapattinam--for longer than he could remember. Today he was in no mood for an extended conversation, but he could not altogether brush off Shahul Hameed.

"These days to get married and to support a family one needs a fortune. The salaries we earn--well you know how far they can be stretched-- and inflation is making things worse each day. I sometimes wonder how married people like you manage."

"One just learns to be thrifty."

"I, suppose one can only pray for a prize in the Social Welfare lottery."

"Lottery? Ah yes, lottery."

Aboo Bakar Maraicar felt his hand going towards his pocket, but he restrained it. He wondered if Shahul Hameed knew that he had won a prize. No. Highly unlikely, he concluded, for he had told no one. He looked around at others seated at the table as if to ascertain if anyone knew. He was certain that the reference to a lottery prize by Shahul Hameed was altogether coincidental and had nothing to do with the ticket he had, secure in his pocket. He did not doubt that in time the word would be out, but as of now, he wanted no one to know.

Aboo Bakar Maraicar washed his right hand in the plate and wiped it on a soiled rag which lay on the table. He was full. The lunch was food, but both the thought of the ticket in his pocket and the conversation with Shahul Hameed had deprived him of some of the pleasures of the meal.

"What does it matter?" he thought to himself. There will be other Fridays for *beriani* and with his prize money he could afford *beriani* everyday at the best eating houses in Madras.

"No, Allah forgive me. I did not intend to be arrogant."

Aboo Bakar genuinely regretted his thought. He must be modest; most of all in his thoughts, for thoughts can be really dangerous things, particularly with Satan's instigation. The win was a gift from Allah and he should thank Allah for it while asking for guidance as to how the money should be spent. He had no right to become proud or arrogant. That would be sinful.

"What's the hurry *Annai?*" It was Nagore Maideen's voice.

"Nothing. Nothing in particular. I just have to go back and write a couple of letters," he lied. In the present circumstance a lie such as that was necessary. He was sure God would understand. He bid a general farewell to all at the restaurant.

"*Assalaamu Alaikum.*"

"*Wa Alaikum Salaam,*" came the response from several of the regular eaters at Jabbarullah's shop. Aboo Bakar lit a *beedi* and left the premises, for he was in a genuine hurry.

Emerging into the blistering afternoon sun, Aboo Bakar Maraicar walked as casually as he could towards Beach Street. He felt awkward, wondering if the casual onlookers noticed anything strange about him. He did not wish to convey the impression to anyone that he had something urgent to handle. The throbbing in his temples became almost unbearable. His mouth felt dry.

Aboo Bakar soon reached the entrance of the United Asian Bank, Beach Street branch. He stood outside the glass door which, as it opened and closed, allowed the coolness of the air-conditioned interior out in whiffs which struck Aboo Bakar. He became hesitant, not daring to push the glass door leading into the cool interior, and to a world of riches. He puffed heavily on his *beedi,* the third since lunch. Ghulam Mustapha & Sons had an account at this particular branch of the United Asian Bank. He had at some time or other met some of its clerks. He even had a nodding acquaintance with the manager, Mr. K. Viswanathan. No doubt Mr.Viswanathan would still remember him, vaguely, if he introduced himself.

But all of a sudden Aboo Bakar Maraicar began to have doubts about cashing his ticket at the United Asian Bank. No, he decided. That would be a certain way of letting people know that he had won a prize worth $25,000.00. Tamil Indians--Hindus and Muslims alike--were, as a race, addicted to gossip. This he knew for a certainty. Thus if he did cash his ticket at the United Asian Bank, chances were the word would soon leak out through the bank clerks. For a while he was confused, uncertain of himself.

He decided to take a walk, think again, and come back in a few minutes. There was still time before the banks closed for business. He even thought of the possibility of settling the matter the next day, but then realized that this would probably cause him even greater anxiety. He would have the added agony of having to ensure the safety of his ticket. No, he must get the matter settled once and for all this very day.

During the following few minutes, while pretending to look at the textiles, the cassettes, the foreign currencies and a host of other articles displayed at the shops and stalls along Beach Street, he made a decision that it would be unwise to return to the United Asian Bank. There were too many Indian workers there, and too many Indian customers to boot. It would be safer to find a bank at which he was completely unknown.

Right across from where he was standing at the corner of Beach Street and Union Street near Barkath Stores stood the old grey building of Chartered Bank. Yes, it would have to be the Chartered Bank, rather than some local one owned by Chinese businessmen. There would be greater security, perhaps better service at a bank which, though now operated by locals, inherited a British tradition.

Crossing the street, Aboo Bakar Maraicar stood at the Beach Street entrance to the bank. There was a crowd inside. Perhaps because it was Friday; perhaps because the banks would be closing soon for the day. He wondered how many of the bank's customers had come to cash lottery tickets. He felt awkward, dressed in his white *sarung* and cream coloured *baju Melayu,* his white *kepiah haji* still on his head. But he had little choice. He had to go in. Summoning enough courage, and taking off his *kepiah haji,* thus exposing his balding head, he entered the stately old building. He approached the burly Sikh security guard with the name tag Bachan Singh. Bachan Singh has a graying beard and there was an air of seriousness about him. Aboo Bakar approached him after some hesitation.

"Bhaii Saahib, where is the Manager's office?"

"You wish to meet the Manager?" Bachan Singh looked up and down at Aboo Bakar as if to assess his worthiness as a customer. The latter felt small and uncomfortable beside Bachan Singh.

"Y. . .yes, Bhai Saahib."

"First go to counter no.4, and talk to the lady there."

Bachan Singh pointed in the direction of a counter where several customers were lined up.

"Thank you Bhai Saahib." He felt nervous. He knew that Bachan Singh was probably still staring at him as he moved away. He wished all this was not necessary. But the matter of the ticket had to be settled before the bank closed at 3.00 p.m. He too had to be back at work at that hour. It was already 2.25 on the Chartered Bank's ancient clock.

Approaching counter no. 4 he joined the short queue, making a strange figure amongst the others in his *sarung* and *baju Melayu*, his *kepiah haji* held in his left like a book.

"Pak Cik, can I help you?" It was his turn.

"Cik, I would like to meet the manager." He managed to half stammer the words, while wondering if the young and pretty short-haired lady behind the counter was Malay, Chinese or Eurasian. Her name tag read Roslina.

"The Manager, Pak Cik?"

"Yes, Cik."

"About what?"

"Something private," Cik."

"Private?"

"Yes."

He wished the interrogation would end. The whole thing was really getting on his nerves.

"I see. Alright. Muthu, Muthu." She called an attendant in a khaki uniform like that of the security guard. She directed Muthu to guide Aboo Bakar to the manager's office.

"You can follow him, Pak Cik."

"Thank you very much, Cik."

He was certain the clerks at the United Asian Bank were not as gentle, soft-spoken or helpful as Roslina. He was glad he decided to enter the Chartered Bank instead. Soon he found himself at the door to the Manager's office. After knocking twice, the attendant pushed the door. Aboo Bakar found himself looking at a rather drab and unimpressive room. Behind a large table sat a flabby bespectacled Chinese man of about fifty.

"Yes?"

"This gentleman would like to meet you, Tuan."

"Yes, come in Encik" said the Manager, without even looking up at Aboo Bakar, who made his way to the table.

"Please take a seat. Give me just a minute while I finish signing these documents."

This time the Manager looked at Aboo Bakar. A plaque on the table indicated his name--Lee Kam Chye. Aboo Bakar sat down, uncomfortable. Completing the documents. Lee Kam Chye rang his table bell. The attendant came in again.

"Please take these to Encik Chong." The documents were handed to the attendant.

"Yes, Encik, what can we do for you?"

"Tuan... Tuan, its like this" My name is Aboo Bakar... Aboo Bakar Maraicar and. . . and . . ." He struggled for words.

"Yes, what is it, Encik Aboo Bakar?"

"It's about...about a lottery ticket..."

"Lottery ticket?"

"Yes, Tuan. You see, I checked in the Tamil newspaper this morning. I have the ticket which won a consolation prize."

"Ah I see, I see. You won a prize in the Social Welfare Lottery."

"Yes, Tuan."

"Congratulations, Encik Aboo Bakar."

"Tuan, I don't know how to go about..."

"I understand, You want to get the ticket cashed, is that it?"

"Yes, Tuan."

"No problem. That should be easy enough . . ."

Aboo Bakar felt relieved. Things were working out rather well. He had always admired the efficiency of the Chinese even though, as a race, he was not particularly fond of them. He was glad he had entered the Chartered Bank.

"You can bring the ticket to us and we will send it for encashment. It will take a few days."

"A few days?"

"Yes, Encik Aboo Bakar, that's quite normal. But don't worry. We will give you an official receipt, and when the money is ready for collection, we will inform you."

"You will contact me?"

"Yes, we will write to you or, if you can give us your telephone number, we can call you."

Aboo Bakar was getting worried again. He was wondering if the ticket would be safe, if he could trust the Manager. He had no doubts that the Chartered Bank was alright, but what about the manager? After all he was Chinese. All this confusion about writing to him or calling him by telephone--somehow it seemed rather complicated.

"Don't worry, Encik Aboo Bakar. Everything will be alright. That's the normal procedure."

"Yes, Tuan."

"Well then, bring the ticket in and we will do the rest for you."

"I have the ticket with me right now, Tuan."

"Good. Then, we can start the process straight away."

Aboo Bakar hesitated for a moment; looked at the manager as if trying to gauge him. Mr. Lee did not appear to be amused.

"Well, would you like us to do it for you? Or do you need more time to think about it? You know, there is no other way in which you can cask the ticket except through a bank."

He sensed the irritation in Mr. Lee's voice.

"Perhaps you had better think about it first, Encik Aboo Bakar. You can always come back tomorrow or next week, if you wish."

"No. no, let it be today. Let it be today, Tuan."

"Good. Can I have your ticket and your identity card, please." He rang his table bell again.

"Muthu, please call Encik Chong for me."

Aboo Bakar's head was spinning with a mixture of excitement and anxiety; excitement at the prospect of at last being able to cash the ticket; anxiety at the thought that he was leaving it in the hands of total strangers, a couple of Chinese men at that.

The cashier, a jovial man of about forty-five came in, and sat on a chair next to the one Aboo Bakar was occupying. Encik Lee explained to Encik Chong the nature of the business at hand. Encik Chong shook hands with Aboo Bakar, his jovial nature effusing from him. Aboo Bakar felt concerned, but forced a smile, now that he had little choice in the matter. Things had begun to work too fast, for him. He seemed to be losing control of the situation.

Aboo Bakar Maraicar uttered a silent *Bismillah* and putting his hand into his *Baju Melayu* pocket, felt for the ticket. A sudden chill went through his spine; his head reeled with panic. He felt again, removed everything from his pockets--his identity card, some cash in notes and loose coins, his room keys, an aerogramme he had received a few days earlier from his daughter Ayesha--but there was no sign of the ticket. Perhaps he had moved it into his upper pocket. He hoped and prayed that this was the case; that he had been mistaken about his pocket.

The search for the ticket in the upper pocket proved equally futile. There was nothing in the upper pocket.

"Ya Allah, where have I put it?"

"What happened, Encik Aboo Bakar?" this time it was Encik Chong.

"I . . . I can't find my ticket."

"Perhaps you put in your purse, or left it at home."

"No, I...I had it with me. I...I had it with me, in this pocket, in this very pocket. O my God. What could have happened to it? What could have happened?" The last part of this utterance came out in Tamil.

Aboo Bakar Maraicar's voice turned into an almost inaudible hiss. His eyes brimmed with tears; he shut them and a teardrop found its way down his right cheek. Placing his arms on the Manager's table, he rested his throbbing head. He was sobbing like a child.

Realising that the business with Aboo Bakar Maraicar was not going to materialise, Encik Lee Kam Chye began to dial a number.

"Hello, hello. Encik Desmond Tan, please."

Comforting Aboo Bakar by patting him on his back several times, Encik Chong left the room. It was getting close to three o'clock.

Soon after the *azan* for *maghrib* prayers, when Aboo Bakar Maraicar regained consciousness he found himself in the third class ward of the Penang General Hospital.

He had no idea why he was in hospital, and how he had found his way there.

MAK YONG DANCER

Leaving my Toyota Corolla at the village store, I must have walked for half an hour that morning looking for the house, passing through the whole *kampung* on foot and across the muddy canal by a narrow wooden slab that served as a bridge not far from the almost treeless graveyard. The grass and *lalang* had grown around the graves, so that some of the older ones, almost totally flattened, were not quite visible, obscured both by time and new vegetation. Only the few granite or cement tombstones, moss-covered, remained standing here and there, the plaster peeling off, the names on them extinguished a long time ago; the wooden ones had begun to show signs of decay or had totally disintegrated. This older section of the graveyard near the canal had apparently been abandoned for some time now; it had become too full. The cemetery had expanded into **an** adjacent coconut land, and the newer graves could be seen at its further end.

I enlisted the assistance of a group of four young children, a boy and three girls, playing in the open space in the coconut plantation, to locate the house. From a distance, when the house first came into view, it was as if it was totally surrounded by the primeval forest, the trees rising high to touch the skies. A few *nangka* trees eventually came into view, as did coconut palms and a cluster of banana trees. A family of fowl foraged for food in the loose brown sand.

The zinc-roofed wooden house itself, in style like most in Kampung Mesira, was old and dilapidated, giving the impression that it had been abandoned and would collapse at any moment. Here and there, planks in the wall were missing and their place had been taken by strips of canvas or unbleached cloth. I wondered if the old woman was still in the house or, as it seemed to me, had moved. The children assured me she was at home. She never went anywhere.

"*Assalamu Alaikum. Assalamu Alaikum.* Mak Su, Mak Su." There was no response. The children joined in.

"*Nenek. Nenek.* Nek. Must be sleeping. Maybe we should knock on the door."

Without waiting for instructions from me, two of the children, perhaps nine or ten years in age, quickly clambered up the five steps to the landing and began to knock. They and their two slightly younger companions, who had remained on the ground, at the same time, maintained their chorus of "Nenek. Nenek. Nek."

A cough and then a voice asked them to wait. I was relieved that she was indeed at home. The children, realising that they could now leave me alone with the old woman, began to shuffle away, gently pushing or pulling each other. I called them back, placed a *ringgit* each in their tiny palms, and then told them to go and continue their games. Their eyes lit up; they looked at each other in wonderment, and then at me, smiling broadly. Then, they began a new chorus.

"*Terima kasih, Pak Cik. Terima kasih Pak Cik.*"

Pocketing their newly-earned wealth, and talking loudly, they were soon on their way back to where I had met them, or perhaps to the local *kedai* to spend the money they had so deservedly earned. It took a while, but at last the sound of the bolt came; the door opened slowly.

"Hai, siapa dia tu?

"Assalamu Alaikum, Mak Su."

"Wa Alaikum Salaam."

I reached up the landing, grasped her frail, shaky hands with my own, held them in my palms for a while, and then raised mine to my chest. Her hands were cold. I told her that I had come from Kuala Lumpur to talk to her about *mak yong;* that I had been given her name by Pak Lah or Dollah Supang, as he was better known by Pak Nik Hassan, the rebab player, as well as by several others.

"Oh, Dollah Supang — How is he? Is he still healthy? And Nik Hassan? It has been years . . ."

"Che Dollah is healthy and active as ever. He sends his salaams. Pak Nik Hassan is growing old and weak. But he still plays the rebab occasionally." She smiled — a nostalgic smile.

"Yes, we are all growing old." And following a pause, she added, "No one plays the rebab like Nik Hassan."

Mak Su was clad in only an old *batik sarung* and had a towel over her shoulders. She was small built, frail, with the slight hint of a hunch, thin and wiry. Her uncombed hair was almost totally grey, but there was a striking glow in her fair face, particularly when she smiled her almost-toothless smile. It was obvious that the stories about how beautiful she had been in her youth were not at all exaggerated. Even now, at perhaps seventy-five, she retained some of that beauty, as well as a certain dignity.

She was barely able to stand. I held her hands, asked her to sit down.

"Come in, come inside," she invited, "Why are you standing on the landing?"

"Never mind, Mak Su. I'll just sit here. It's quite pleasant outside."

"Wait, then. I'll get a mat."

The surroundings of the house were altogether agreeable, with the sounds of birds and the cool gentle morning breeze rustling through the leaves, bringing in the thousand-year-old smell of the forest. I wondered why the house was cut off from the rest of the kampung.

Mak Su brought an old mat, and spread it out on the landing floor. She asked me to sit, and then went back into the house, saying she would take only a little while. When she returned a few minutes later, she had tied up her hair in a bun, put on a faded *baju kurung* and appeared altogether more appropriately prepared to meet her unexpected visitor. She had brought with her a tray with a pot of *kopi-O*, a bunch of bananas, two glasses, some not-so-fresh *sirih* leaves with the ingredients, as well as a betel-nut pounder. I helped her place the tray on the mat, and she sat down, leaning against the wall near the door-mouth.

"Sorry, there's nothing at home to eat except last night's rice."

"Just coffee will do, Mak Su. Thank you very much for your trouble."

"So you came all this distance from Kuala Lumpur just to see me, my son?"

"Yes, Mak Su. You see, I have been studying mak yong for several months now. During my previous visits, I met many of the performers, mostly younger ones, but some veterans too." Mak Su was intrigued.

"So you are learning to perform mak yong?" She asked with a smile that I thought was deliberately mischievous and a glint in her eye.

"No, No." I laughed. "I'm only doing interviews, and will perhaps write something about mak yong and about well-known performers like you when I have enough information. You see, I work for a newspaper. I am a journalist."

"Why do you want to want to write about mak yong? Nobody is interested in these things. They will all fade away. Even now, few perform it in the old style. I am sure you already know that."

"Yes, Mak Su. I know it has changed a great deal, but we should at least gather whatever information we can still get regarding its authentic style and its history before it dies out altogether. There is much that is fascinating in it. That is why I am here. Its only people like you who preserve, in their memories as well as in their bodies, much of what is important in mak yong — its myths and legends, its music and songs, how it was performed in the villages and in the palace."

"If one is interested, of course, there is a great deal to discover. Mak yong is a deep ocean. But how many people are interested in these ancient things? You see, *anak*, there's nothing like mak yong. Few realise what it is and what it has the power to do. Through mak yong, you see the immortal dance of nature. In mak yong, you hear the voice of God."

She lapsed into singing in a low voice. I recognised words from the opening song of mak yong performances, *Lagu Mengadap Rebab*, and her hands began to move in a slow dance:

Like the elephant swaying its trunk
Like the wild jungle fowl preparing for battle
"That's beautiful, Mak Su."

She still had a beautiful voice. I wished I had brought my cassette recorder; I made a mental note not to leave it behind in my hotel room if I ever came this way again.

"There are not many around with *jiwa seni*, an artistic soul. People have become so materialistic, they don't appreciate true beauty these days, much less beauty in the voice and in words. Even good mak yong singers have become a rarity."

The intense beauty of mak yong, manifested particularly in its dance and music, was unquestionable. Its spiritual side had been hinted to me many times before by other performers. But no one was prepared to go beyond the basics. Was it at all possible that, at last, through Mak Su I would reach deeper into the soul of mak yong?

My chest began to brim with excitement as my breathing changed pace, as if in anticipation of something far from the ordinary. I wished I had more time to spend with Mak Su. I resolved that in the event it was necessary, I would return again, and again, and yet again to reach into the deep ocean which had begun to open itself out to receive me. But this time, I could not spend more than perhaps a day or two longer unless I made special arrangements to extend my leave.

For now, it had to be just Mak Su Zainab and her story, the story of a single artistic soul. She began to tell me about the rebab and its meaning; she told me that of all instruments, it was the rebab which came closest to the human voice.

"One can sense the sadness and the joy in its voice, especially when played by someone like Nik Hassan."

Soon, she became silent, turning her attention to the *sirih pinang*, pounding on the betel nuts. She prepared a quid and began to chew it, making noise with her almost toothless mouth, wiping with her palm the saliva that had begun to trickle.

That gave me a break for a cigarette, and for a cup of coffee. I also prepared my camera for a few shots of Mak Su. Fearing that she would object, I decided not to seek her permission, just took it for granted that she would have no objection. When I moved down the landing to get some portraits, she was more than willing to pose, making herself erect, and adjusting her clothes, seated on the *lantai* as she was, smiling.

"What do you need pictures of an old crone like me for?" she asked. "You should have seen some of those they took of me during my younger days. But they are all gone. Taken by people."

Unfortunately, she had no pictures left; she could not even tell me positively who had them, and if ever I could see some of them. But this was the opportunity I was waiting for: to turn the discussion around to her person.

As the discussion continued, its focus already shifting, I took the opportunity to develop this side of the interview — Mak Su as an individual and as a performer. That would give my article a degree of originality, reflecting the uniqueness of this intriguing woman.

"I was told you were an active performer in the *istana* together with Dollah Supang, Pak Nik Hassan, Cik Kemala and so on?"

"Yes, in Kampung Temenggung; not really in the *balai*. We never performed in the palace. Before the Second World War, before the great Red Flood, Air Bah Merah."

That great flood had taken place in 1926. She told me that she had, in fact, been performing mak yong since the very early age in the villages, in a troupe headed by her parents — her father was a well-known rebab player and her mother an outstanding *pak yong* performer. Later, she herself became a serious actress at the very early age of fifteen. When plans to develop a mak yong troupe in Kampung Temenggung were initiated, recruiting teams were sent to the villages and she was one of those selected. Her parents too were invited to Kampung Temenggung, but they were there just for two weeks. She stayed on. At that time, she was seventeen.

Hers had been a large family, since her father, originally from Sungei Golok in Thailand, had married several times. But all her brothers and sisters had passed away with the exception of two half-sisters who, upon marriage had gone off to other districts of

Kelantan. Mak Su Zainab herself became the seventh wife of a prince just a year after she reached Kampung Temenggung.

"You must have been very beautiful."

"I was young, and could perform mak yong well — the singing, the dancing —that was what attracted the prince to me. He had a genuine interest in these things. Later, he made me an instructor and then one day he asked me for my hand in marriage. What could I say? How could I refuse? The prince was old. But since he had decided he wanted me, there was nothing I could do but go along with his wishes. At that time, he had three other living wives, and could take on a fourth. It was quite common, and even now in Kelantan this goes on, as you probably know. After all you are a journalist."

Kampung Temenggung had not lasted long. It came to an end with the Prince himself going away, never to return. Some stories maintain that he went to a deserted island; became a recluse. And then the war had broken out. I asked her what happened.

"When the Kampung Temenggung troupe closed down, I continued performing mak yong in the villages with my parents and other troupes. For many, many years and in all the districts of Kelantan, I performed mak yong, travelling with my father's troupe from one *pesta* to another, from one village to another. I became quite well-known."

She had remarried after several years, but the marriage ended in divorce. From a third marriage, she had three children, two of whom had already died, and several grandchildren. Her last husband had died more than twelve years ago. She was supported by her one surviving son and several grandsons.

"You see, my husband owned some coconut land in this neighbourhood, but most of it got sold off, and then, by the time he died we had nothing. He was a *kaki joget* and a womaniser; spent much of his money on frivolous things.

"And this house? Does it belong to you?"

"No. No. No. No. I live here due to the kindness of the Tok Penghulu. He owns the land around this house. But it did belong to my husband once."

That, briefly, was her personal history as she told me in a nutshell.

An hour and a half had passed since I began talking to Mak Su Zainab. I needed a break and I certainly thought she would benefit from one. I did not wish to strain her. Had she indicated even in the vaguest of terms that she could not proceed I would have stopped. I told her that I would go for a short walk.

The basic information had begun to trickle out of Mak Su. But for me, the more important questions remained. These had essentially to do with the inner aspects of mak yong as seen from her own perspective. I hoped that after the short rest some success could be attained in this direction too. I did not, of course, wish to deceive myself into believing that anything worthwhile could be achieved in a single day of interviews.

Mak Su had been helpful to the extreme, following the establishment of almost immediate rapport between us. I am certain the names of Che Dollah Supang and others had been veritable passports for me. They had always been. And Mak Su's spirits had been raised. I hoped that they would remain sufficiently high for me to continue with the interview after an early lunch. I did not wish to push her. I had to wait and see how things went. I still had two days in Kota Bharu and could easily return to see her the following day if necessary.

I returned an hour later with two packets of *nasi dagang*, some fruits, a tin of biscuits as well as two cans of Sprite, which I could very well use, given that the day was getting hotter. I did not think she would want a bottled drink. Mak Su was overwhelmed, gave me a hug. I could feel her bones.

Following lunch, Mak Su desired some rest. So I waited on the landing, and later decided that I too would lie down for a while. Although it was getting warmer, the forest trees and the vegetation, coupled with the gentle late morning breeze conspired to create an altogether congenial atmosphere. I began to formulate further questions I would ask Mak Su.

These would focus, I decided, on her ancestry, her initiation into mak yong, and her spiritual training. I had no illusions. It was very likely that I would not get any further than I had in the morning; most of these topics were rarely discussed by mak yong practitioners, even with close friends. I was not only an outsider but also belonged to a different race. During previous visits to Kelantan, I had been told that, several years before me, two *Orang Putih* had done some interviews with mak yong and wayang kulit practitioners; these had taken place in the Kota Bharu Rest House. I knew who they were and had read some of their brief accounts. I may have been the first Malaysian ever, Malay or non-Malay to talk to Mak Su Zainab about mak yong.

The next thing I knew was that I had awakened from an hour-long sleep. It was *Zuhur* time, and in the totally bare interior of the house, whose sole outstanding feature was the mosquito-net, Mak Su was praying, seated on a prayer-mat and facing an open window, the light giving a soft white glow to her face and *telukung*-covered body. I went to the simple bathroom built around a well at the back of the house to refresh myself.

"You should have slept inside, Anak. It's cooler."

Mak Su emerged. I merely said that it was really quite pleasant outside, with the breeze. She brought some coffee, and when she had

settled down on the mat-covered floor, I asked if she was ready to
continue our discussion. She nodded several times, smiling.

I had always been intrigued by the question of connections
between traditional artists and their predecessors. Mak Su told me
in extremely brief terms that her family in fact hailed from a long
line of mak yong performers.

"You know, they say we are actually connected with the Patani
royal family." She laughed. "I don't know if it is true. It seems one
of my great-great-great grandfathers was a prince and also a fine
musician during the time of Raja Hijau, the Queen of Patani. But
you know each one of the sultans and princes had several wives and
many, many children. Not all could become kings." She laughed
again. "And so here we are today, like this, with nothing to live on.
We can only become kings and queens in mak yong performances;
even become gods, *dewa*; it's all a matter of pretence."

"Do you believe the story?"

"I don't know what to say. But it is possible. That is why I have
this *angin*."

"Angin?" And I wondered what mak yong had to do with the
breezes that blew pleasantly around us as we sat on the lantai. I
unconsciously turned my gaze towards the trees, and she must have
guessed my thoughts.

"No, no, not those kinds of angin. I am talking about internal
winds – *angin mak yong*, *angin joget* and so many other angin. They
are connected with the *jiwa*, the soul."

I was intrigued but I did not want to trouble Mak Su or get
confused myself. I noted that angin was something to discuss with
her or with other mak yong people on some later occasion. For
now, I merely assumed it was the same or had something to do
with possessing an artistic spirit — *jiwa seni* — or at least with a
performer's soul.

"Yes, I see what you mean. So, how did you get started in mak yong, Mak Su? Did it come naturally to you or did it take a special effort on your part to get involved?"

"At first I did not get involved, although my mother tried very hard to get me to learn and also to perform. And then, strange things began to happen. I became very ill; lost all mood to eat, drink, sleep or to work. My parents took me to consult several *bomoh* and doctors, the best in Kelantan, but to no avail. I became so thin it looked as if I would shrivel to death. And then, one night, my dreams began. I would, again and again, see this shadowy image of an old person, so doubly bent over that it was impossible to tell whether he or she was a male or female. Reminded me of Semar, the ancient Javanese god and clown. My parents told me he was some venerable ancestor — could it have been the Patani prince? But if so, why did he assume such an amorphous form, I wondered. Or, of course, it could have been Semar himself, my father added. The visitor in my dreams would say a few words, words I could not make out, and then he would suddenly be wiped off the screen. Each time he came and went with a strange golden light. One night, he told me I should go hunting for a white deer; he called me Dewa Muda."

"Dewa Muda, the character from the mak yong play?"

"Yes, that very same."

"So what happened next?

"My uncle, who was a well-known *main puteri* bomoh in the village and also a mak yong performer, interpreted the dream to mean that I had to perform mak yong, doing the story of Dewa Muda, so that I could be cured of my illness. There was no other way out. Still I resisted, and my condition became worse. In desperation, with my parents' consent, my uncle arranged for a main puteri performance combined with mak yong. Can you believe it; they had to carry me to the stage, like a corpse? I was made to lie on a mat."

"Did you know what was going on?"

"I was in a state of total confusion; only vaguely aware of what was happening. The music sent me into a strange state of mind. I was in between the real and the unreal. The main puteri was used to ascertain my real problem. It appeared that a particular spirit was preventing me from performing mak yong. That spirit had to be pacified. The following night, a large tray of offerings were prepared for him, and the panggung elaborately decorated. When the main puteri started, no one believed what I did.

"You danced?"

"How did you guess? Yes, I danced, and danced so violently that I could not stop. I was in trance. I was transformed into that spirit that was troubling me. I behaved exactly as he would have had he been in the panggung. In between the dance, I would collapse, rise again and dance; again and again I did that. I cried; cried and cried uncontrollably, like someone gone insane. Others joined in the dance, also in a state of trance. At long last, exhausted, I collapsed on the panggung floor. I slept for hours until late into the morning. When I woke up, I felt much better. A bath in water containing lime and certain offerings, a *mandi pelimau*, further improved my spirits. My uncle chanted some mantera, threw yellow rice on me to further assist in the cure. The depression seemed to have gone, and believe me; it never came back again, never, in any serious way.

On the third night, very elaborate offerings had been prepared for the gods and spirits. There were some further rituals. Following those, dressed in complete pak yong costume, I performed a short scene from *Dewa Muda*, imitating my mother at every step, as she danced and sang on the panggung. You know, she was very beautiful; she also had a really good voice. And that's how I became a mak yong performer."

"How fascinating …without any formal training."

"Not exactly."

Mak Su Zainab paused for a while, put a quid of betel leaves and pounded betel nuts into her mouth, and chewed.

"Following an initiation, I formally accepted my mother as my teacher. Her mantle so to speak, fell, against my choice, upon my weak and humble shoulders. This had been dictated by Semar Hitam, as well as by the spirit of the old royal ancestor who first played music in the court of Raja Hijau. The big advantage has been that I have rarely been ill again, and even if I did feel unwell, a mak yong performance, its dance or just its songs seemed to revive me. That does not mean that I have not been ill at all. I have had, of course, to see doctors for certain physical illnesses; such illnesses lie outside the realm of main puteri or mak yong."

There was much that I had learnt from this one conversation with Mak Su. But my desire to delve further into the field had been kindled with the meeting. The day was stretching towards evening, and it was approaching to *Maghrib* time. I felt that I should leave Mak Su Zainab now, so that she could have some rest from the strain of talking to me the whole day long.

"When will you come to see me again?"

"I'm not sure, Mak Su, but I will certainly try."

"Please do come. Come tomorrow or the day after. Any time before you leave for Kuala Lumpur."

I knew that this was both an invitation and a command. I promised Mak Su that I would be back to see her not the next day, but the day after that, about the same time in the morning. She seemed very glad. I shook hands with her in the traditional style, with both hands, but in my hand I had placed a hundred ringgit note, which I pressed her to take. Her lips pouted as if she was about to weep. She hugged me once again, and as soon as she released me, unable to contain my own emotion, I was on my way back to my car.

Two days later, when I reached Mak Su Zainab's house early in the morning, I was better prepared. I had brought with me my tape-recorder, some blank cassettes, even an old cassette recording of part of a mak yong performance done by a well-known currently active troupe, which I had been listening to on my car tape-recorder. I would leave this behind with Mak Su. I had also brought Mak Su a bouquet of flowers.

"Assalaamu Alaikum, Mak Su."

"Wa Alaikum Salaam."

Dressed in new clothes, as well as some simple jewellery, and properly groomed, Mak Su looked even more radiant this time than she had two days before. I sat on the breezy mat-covered lantai as before, and she brought out kopi-O which had already been prepared. There were also several pieces of *kuih* and *pisang goreng*. I presented her with the flowers, much to her delight. She smelt them for a moment and then put them on the floor inside the door, pulling out just a single flower in full bloom, to place in her neatly tied hair.

We drank coffee. In my mind, I had begun to frame some further questions to ask her when, as I expected, the interview continued after coffee.

"Ah, you have a tape recorder. Good. I thought we could use my old one. It is more than twenty years old; it still works. But yours will be better."

I was wondering what she had in mind. Perhaps, she was going to listen to the recording I had just given her. She stood up, held my hand and asked me to follow her into the interior of the house. I did not resist; taking my tape recorder with me, I followed her. There was no furniture. The mosquito-net covered a mattress, and, hanging on the wall from a hook was a rebab enclosed in its cloth jacket. I would ask her to let me have a look at it later on.

I sat on a mat; she brought me a cassette, pulled out of a trunk. It must have been at least ten years old.

"Here, play this."

Mak Su sat cross-legged in front of me. I dusted the cassette, loaded it into my player, and pressed the "play" button. From it issued the strains of a rebab, and when the tune began, I immediately recognised it — Lagu Mengadap Rebab.

And then the most incredible thing happened. Mak Su listened, intensely, to the music, her eyes half-shut, as she swayed gently from side to side. Next, at the appropriate instant, began the slow motions of *tari mengadap rebab* the opening dance of mak yong. It was her voice on the cassette recorder, the song recorded with full mak yong musical accompaniment. I became totally mesmerised, both by the sounds and by the infinitely subtle movements as Mak Su Zainab, full of such energy as no one would have believed she possessed, executed to perfection, sitting on the floor, standing on three points and finally standing up and moving in a languorous circle. I do not know where the energy came from.

As the dance progressed, Mak Su was transformed from a frail old *mak cik* into someone no more than eighteen years of age, a dancer in the court of Raja Hijau of Patani, an *apsara* in Indra's heaven. And I became Indra himself. My eyes shut; I remained seated on the floor, swaying gently from side to side, my hands held together on my lap, long after the dance had stopped, long after the music had ended.

"What happened? Have you fallen asleep?"

"No, Mak Su, I have been in heaven. I have heard the voice of God."

BIRTHDAY

Suddenly, at the age of forty-eight, Pak Dollah realised he was beginning to grow old. Somehow, up to that time, the process of aging, or rather moving from childhood into adolescence and from adolescence into manhood had taken so natural a course, without mishap, that there had been no real cause for concern.

It happened precisely on the evening of his forty-eighth birthday celebration, to use a conventional phrase, for in Kampung Dodol; birthdays were not celebrated or even remembered in any special way.

The custom of marking birthdays with the burning of candles and the cutting of cakes was one Western tradition increasingly coming into vogue not only among the younger Malaysians, but also, Pak Dollah noted, among the *nouveau riche,* the literate and the powerful. The practice was particularly prevalent among ministers, deputy ministers as well as other VIPs' including senior government officers and politicians. In such cases, he realised, birthday parties had a legitimate function. They were intended to facilitate the enhancing of political influence, of obtaining favours (which, be it noted were mutual, benefiting giver and receiver alike), and, of course, of legitimizing gifts.

Pak Dollah knew of several persons now in the habit of dispensing their influence, receiving gratitude in the form of gifts — hampers, cheques, liquor, cars, trips to Hadyai and even, occasionally, houses

— all in the name of birthday celebrations which oftentimes became riotous events, occasions for gambling, intemperance and other more lascivious forms of entertainment.

Pak Dollah celebrated his forty-eighth birthday not in the manner of these *nouveau riche* or influential members of his race, for he belonged to neither of these categories, being a humble headmaster of a small secondary school. It had been a simple *kenduri* with his brothers and sisters, half-brothers and half-sisters, some of his many nephews and nieces and a small pack of grandnephews and grandnieces. As usual, the *Tok Imam* from the nearby Perak Road mosque had been invited to conduct the *doa selamat,* in the pious hope of more such birthdays for Pak Dollah. As was the norm, to keep the affair small and within the family, not even Pak Dollah's colleagues from Sekolah Menengah Datuk Kaya had been invited.

This habit of having a small religious ceremony had been acquired only in recent years. In the past, Pak Dollah used to celebrate his birthdays in other ways, oftentimes with the boisterous friends of his riotous youth, getting together with them in some gaudy Halfway Road bar, or at the Taman Selera where *satay, mee goreng* and Tiger beer served the purpose well enough and did not leave a big hole in his pocket.

And then, over the years, almost imperceptibly, the manner of celebrating birthdays had changed for Pak Dollah into the aforementioned religious ceremony. Some bananas or other fruits would be distributed at the mosque after *isya* prayers and the customary *doa selamat* recited; alternatively, some food would be sent to the Air Itam Muslim Orphanage.

Long since his early youth, Pak Dollah had shunned spirits even though he had spent two years in England as a trainee teacher at Brinsford Lodge. Not that Pak Dollah was particularly pious. He merely saw no reason to waste his hard-earned money on liquor.

Drunkenness, somehow, did not become a cultured and intelligent person, he decided, what more a school-teacher, and a Muslim? And so, naturally, over the past decade or so, when birthdays were celebrated, there was, in them, no place for spirits.

He could not remember precisely when the religious influence had begun thus to creep in. It happened mainly as a result of the advice given by his elder half-brother, Pak Kadir, a pious member of the family of three brothers and seven sisters, the offspring of the ample loins of one father, Tuan Haji Abdul Karim, and three mothers. Tuan Haji Abdul Karim had, by the Grace of Allah, married four times and had issue by three of his wives. The fourth wife he had married rather late in life, at the age of sixty-two; Nor Azlina was then only nineteen.

Two years later, Tuan Haji Abdul Karim had died of heart failure, collapsing in the *mesjid* one evening after *tarawih*. He now lay buried in the over-crowded Perak Road Muslim Cemetery. It is said those who die during the holy month of Ramadan go straight to Heaven, for the gates thither remain open during the entire blessed month. The family of Tuan Haji Abdul Karim had not the slightest doubt that their venerable gentleman had found his way straight into Paradise. May Allah bless his soul and have mercy on us all.

Tuan Haji Abdul Karim's first two wives had already passed away and the third one was close to joining him through terminal cancer. Nor Azlina, however, was still rather strikingly attractive at the age of twenty-nine. She had decided not to remarry (at least for the time being) although it was common knowledge she was the constant companion of Mansor Ahmad Osman, the manager of a thriving Malay finance company, Cepumas Inderawangsa Sdn Bhd. Indeed, it was fairly consistently heard on the grapevine that the relationship was a more than casual one despite the fact that Mansor Ahmad was already married. It was he who provided Nor

Azlina with the finance to start her Batik Boutique in the lobby of a well-known Batu Feringhi hotel. The terms of transaction remain unknown despite much guessing in Kampung Dodol.

Pak Kadir became pious of a sudden after the demise of Tuan Haji Abdul Karim. He followed his father's well-marked footsteps. He had performed the Hajj to Mecca, and had himself married a second time only recently to a woman much younger to him. This, he affirmed, was the Will of God, and if Allah willed he should marry a third, or even a fourth wife, then he would do so, *Insha Allah*. His two wives concurred with him. Nothing could come in the way of God's Will.

Pak Dollah could not remember exactly how many birthdays he had celebrated in this religious manner: five, six, perhaps eight at the most. But of all his birthdays, the forty-eighth remained the most significant. It marked a turning point in Pak Dollah's life.

That night, after the *kenduri*, Pak Dollah was about to retire. Suddenly, when ascending the short flight of stairs, he felt giddy, and had a blackout. He was unable to control himself and his attempts to catch hold of a banister failed. He fell and rolled down onto the ground. Those members of the family who rushed in to investigate found Pak Dollah sprawled on the ground, breathing heavily and perspiring, his clothes dirty, his *songkok* and spectacles lying some distance away.

They carried him upstairs. Someone fanned him with a *mengkuang* leaf fan. Someone else was rubbing *minyak angin* on his forehead and temples. The mixed aromas of mengkuang and minyak angin assailed his senses.

He could hear several anxious voices, intermingled and undistinguishable. Numerous questions flew at high speed in his direction. But for some time, Pak Dollah was in no condition to make any sensible response. Gradually, as the feeling of giddiness and the initial shock left him, the various voices acquired identity, gathered meaning. Had he had a heart attack? Pak Dollah merely shook his head from side to side. No. At least, that was what he thought. Was it appendicitis or a gastric attack? Each time his head shook from side to side. Thus, many of the more dramatic of all likely ailments were dismissed one by one before the arrival of Dr. Ranganatha to whom one of Pak Dollah's nephews had taken a message driving Pak Dollah's old Morris Minor 1000.

The examination confirmed that there had been no heart attack. There was no sign of cardiac trouble. This came as a relief to members of his family, although some, as is typical in these circumstances, felt they did not need a doctor to tell them so. They had already decided upon that long before Dr. Ranganatha's arrival. The doctor similarly ruled out all other serious ailments. He could find nothing wrong with Pak Dollah except mild hypertension which, he surmised, could have caused a giddy spell. Since Pak Dollah's hypertensive condition was not a persistent one, however, Dr. Ranganatha did not wish at that point to start any specific treatment for it. He merely advised his patient to rest, to have some regular exercise, and to bring his weight down. Standing five feet four inches on his bare feet, Pak Dollah weighed one hundred and seventy-five pounds.

When most members of the family, upon learning that there was no immediate danger, had left Pak Dollah's room talking among themselves in excited, articulate whispers, Dr. Ranganatha advised Pak Dollah to cut down some of his sexual activities as he was no longer young. This immensely enraged Pak Dollah. Although he felt like punching the doctor right on his nose, he remained calm, so as not to draw on any unnecessary and unpleasant attention to himself. Dr. Ranganatha merely winked. 27.00 ringgit.

The last bit of Dr. Ranganatha's advice however amused several of those who chanced to overhear it. Some were positive the doctor could not have meant his remark to be taken seriously. Why, Pak Dollah wasn't even married. In other minds, the advice triggered imaginings of Pak Dollah's secret liaisons. They concluded that the present illness must indeed be direct consequence of the headmaster's sexual excesses.

There was instant gossip in Kampung Dodol, and a few days later, when Pak Dollah had somewhat recovered, a lecture from Pak Kadir.

"Enough of this lechery," ended his diatribe. "Time for you to get married."

"Lechery?" shouted Pak Dollah. "What lechery?"

Soon, two stories filled the sensitive Kampung Dodol air. First, that Pak Dollah, the headmaster, had had a heart attack because of excessive sex; and second, that Pak Dollah, the headmaster, was looking for a bride. Many in Kampung Dodol got busy in one way or another as a direct result of these stories.

Pak Dollah couldn't stand all this. His anger at the gossip and at Pak Kadir's words only served to further raise his blood pressure. He applied for several days' additional medical leave and took two weeks off from work. After all, the school was about to close for the vacation anyway and the Senior Assistant could bloody well take care of the place. About time he did some work, thought Pak Dollah. Before sunrise one morning, Pak Dollah made himself scarce from Kampung Dodol, driving away into the darkness.

Where he had gone no one knew. Not even those closest to him. Some began to get genuinely concerned, fearing Pak Dollah might end up doing something quite disastrous in his anger. Others felt sorry they had offended him, poor man. Right now, however, no apologies could be tendered despite their utmost sincerity in wanting to apologise. Pak Dollah was nowhere in Kampung Dodol to receive their apologies.

This search for a bride, initiated by several well-meaning betel-munching matchmakers, soon came to a grinding halt. On the question of Pak Dollah's potential marriage too, there was a strong division of opinion. While some felt it would be good for Pak Dollah to tie the nuptial knot without further delay, others took the stand that any hasty quest for a candidate without his consent would only serve to further offend the already aggrieved Pak Dollah.

Pak Dollah, meanwhile, had slipped away into the quiet mists of Pulau Langkawi to do some serious thinking. The cause of his vertigo, he realised, was not even known to himself. Perhaps there was some truth in the doctor's theories about excessive weight and hypertension. But his weight had been constant for many years now. It had never been a problem; then why the sudden giddy spells and blackout? The answer struggled to come forth — he was growing old. But Pak Dollah suppressed it. No, that could not be.

Pak Dollah examined himself, reluctantly, perhaps even unconsciously, in a full-length mirror in his Langkawi Country Club room. He had never before had a good, critical look at himself. Yes, he did look a little over-weight, short and stocky, with a more than slight paunch. Perhaps, he should do some regular walking, even if only in the school grounds during school hours. All he did now was to sit at his desk all day long. Yes, he would reduce his weight by a few pounds. That should make him look trim and a few years younger.

Several strands of greying hair at his temples now attracted his attention. He had never been struck by them before, though he stood in front of a mirror every morning having his shave. Perhaps then, Dr Ranganatha had been right about his being no longer young, except of course, Pak Dollah was quick to add, for that bit about excessive sex. For that, Pak Dollah could not forgive him.

It has been said that a vacant mind is the devil's workshop. A nervous and frightened mind is an equally dangerous animal. The shock Pak Dollah experienced as a result of his fall caused in him a considerable erosion of self-confidence. Perhaps, the doctor had deliberately concealed from him the fact that he did have a heart trouble, so as not to unduly worry him. Perhaps, there was indeed a mild heart condition. This was one direction Pak Dollah's thinking took at this stage.

On the other hand, he also began to wonder if, in fact, there was not something more sinister about the whole thing; if someone was not using *ilmu jahat* to harm him. Not that he was unreasonably superstitious or believed in magic. But such things were known to actually transpire. He tried to reason with himself that such a thing was unlikely. However, once the thought had struck him, it caught on like a leech. He recalled, by turn, all the people with whom he came into regular contact. There were his family members, his colleagues, and a few friends. Enemies? No, he did not have any enemies.

Then, was some woman trying to charm him? To get him to fall in love with her? That could not be. He was aware that love charms generally caused the victim to go irresistibly towards the user of a charm, instead of fleeing. Enchanted persons became virtual slaves of charm-users. So, if any woman had been using charms to entrap him, he could not be sitting alone in Pulau Langkawi enveloped by the sandy loneliness of Tanjung Rhu Beach.

All the same, despite his apparently convincing line of argument, his thoughts drifted to Sekolah Menengah Datuk Kaya. It was possible, he reflected, that one or two women there liked him.

Fatimah binti Hussein, the school clerk seemed always attempting to catch his eye. She invariably touched him casually when she visited him in his private office. He wondered if that was an invitation to do likewise. Whenever she did manage to do so, she smiled gently. He noted that of late, she had started wearing increasingly tight *sarung kebaya,* revealing her well-formed figure to full advantage. The slits in her sarung too seemed to be rising higher. She often lingered longer than was necessary in his office and long after she left, the sensuous smell of perfume and powder would hang in the air. He had never given these things any serious thought before.

Then there was Rosnah, the Mathematics teacher, who also at times seemed to go out of her way to attract his attention. But he knew she had a husband and two young children. He wondered if she was up to any tricks. After all there were rumours of marital rift and impending divorce.

Finally, there was the divorcee, Halimah, at the National Union of Teachers office. He had noticed her peculiar behaviour several times. Did she become thus excited only when he visited the place, he wondered?

Of the three, he decided, if anyone was trying to seduce him, it was Fatimah. He had occasionally flirted with her, but he did not think his actions could be interpreted as signs of encouragement; they were merely intended to establish better rapport. The nature of their work was such that it brought them into constant proximity; there was nothing more to it, he concluded.

Yet, the image of Fatimah lingered long in his mind, mildly exciting him. Perhaps, she was indeed using some form of magic. He decided to establish the truth once and for all; he would visit a *bomoh*. There was a particularly well-known Siamese one, Din Keliang, in Kodiang, close to the Thai-Buddhist temple, *wat* Siam.

Pak Dollah's memory drifted back to his Brinsford Lodge days. He had once been in love with a fellow trainee teacher. Shamsiah was extremely good-looking, fair skinned. He had fallen in love with her right from their first meeting. Somehow, during those two Brinsford years, her presence grew upon him.

They became friends. The unsuspected barrier Pak Dollah encountered was that Shamsiah belonged to royalty. She was Tengku Shamsiah. Would he, as a commoner and a mere school teacher at that, have even the remotest chance of marrying her? Why not? There were many precedents. He spent a great deal of time pondering the status of their relationship. And then, one impatient day, he decided the only way to obtain a clear answer to his dilemma was to propose to her.

This he did, one evening, during an after-dinner stroll. Her response, though perhaps not altogether unexpected, came as a shock to him. She was already engaged to be married, she told him, to Tengku Abdul Aziz, a member of royalty from one of the Malay states. She chastised him for his presumption, for being so blind, for mistaking infatuation for love. Her open, friendly nature he had taken as a sign of love. This was, to her, only a manifestation of his immaturity. He was shattered.

For several weeks, he had no courage to look her in the face. Although after a while Shamsiah somewhat warmed towards him, it was never like before. There was a chasm between them — the gulf between a commoner and true blue-blooded member of royalty.

After Brinsford Lodge, he never saw Shamsiah again. He read in the newspapers of her impending marriage to Tengku Abdul Aziz. The announcement brought to the fore all the pangs on unrequited passion in him. He felt miserable. Surprisingly, he received no invitation card. Would he have gone to the wedding had he been invited? He was not certain. Pak Dollah sent a congratulatory telegram on the occasion of the wedding. He even received a printed note of acknowledgement and thanks from the two royal houses.

For all practical purposes, the relationship ended the night he
had ventured to propose to Shamsiah. In his soul, however, the agony
lingered on. Pak Dollah never really recovered from his obsession
with Shamsiah or the trauma of rejection. He had resolved after the
break with her never again to get involved with any woman. He
idealised the fair-skinned, blue-blooded beauty that Shamisah was.
No one could ever match her.

Perhaps to forget the past, perhaps as a means of taking revenge
against womankind, unthinking, Pak Dollah had completely
abandoned himself for some time to short-term relationships, often
lasting a single night, with various women — mostly massage parlour
girls, bar-waitresses, and coffeehouse hostesses. This too, had been
a short, transitory phase of Pak Dollah's existence. And then, little
by little, he had given up all thoughts of women or marriage. All
his brothers and sisters had married and raised families. Every now
and then, Pak Kadir would suggest he get married. How long did he
plan to live a bachelor? After all, he was not growing any younger.

The clean Langkawi air and the rest he managed to get on
the island helped him recuperate. All he did during the day was to
walk along the beaches, to eat, sleep and read Malay and English
poetry. The passion for poetry had developed in Pak Dollah during
his Brinsford Lodge days, mainly because Shamsiah herself had an
interest in classical Malay poetry. Occasionally, he took short trips
to places connected with the legend of Mahsuri. There were days
when he did not speak to anyone except to waiters and room service
people at the Country Club. The quietness of the island, silent save
for the pounding waves, served to relax him. Wherever his eyes
travelled beyond the sandy fringe, there was nothing save the blue-
green sea and the crisp ultramarine sky, broken here and there by
clouds of intriguing shapes. The setting served to arouse the poetry
in Pak Dollah's soul.

Several issues engaged Pak Dollah's attention during those Langkawi days and nights. For the first time in his life, he began to feel that he was growing old. He wondered how long he was going to live. A Sikh palmist had once predicted he would live to the age of sixty. But how reliable were these itinerant Indian palmists? His sixtieth birthday was only twelve years away. Twelve years was a very, very short length of time, an unseen speck on the long, endless line of eternity. And if the Sikh was at all accurate in his predictions, the Angel of Death would soon come for his soul. He felt nervous, even frightened, thinking thus of the inevitable arrival of Azrael. Yet, life and death were in the hands of God; there was nothing anyone could do about them. Only He, Allah the All-knowing, knew when Pak Dollah would die. It had all been written down.

He pondered long and deep on the question of marriage. Pak Kadir's words, although not altogether true, still rang in his ears. He had avoided the subject for years. Marriage would bring in its wake other problems: a wife and perhaps children. Could he support a family on his income? He wasn't too sure. Even now, as a single person, there were times when he found that his salary of 750.00 *ringgit* per month did not stretch too far. The money seemed to go in a hundred different directions and that too despite his prudence. Perhaps, it was a good thing he had not got married. He had been able to save a little and do some travelling in Singapore, Indonesia and Thailand. He was particularly glad he had taken the opportunity to visit Lake Toba and Phuket. He had been able to invest in a two-roomed single storey terrace house in Bayan Baru. He had escaped all the petty quarrels that inevitably, it seems, form a part of any marriage. His brother, Zakariah and Rosminah, only recently married, were already talking about divorce.

Then again, looking back at his recent fall, and, more reluctantly, at his advancing years, he felt that a wife and family could, perhaps, bring solace in his old age when he was no longer able to take care of himself. In the place of his loneliness, perhaps a marriage could bring some love and happiness. And what did he work so hard for if he was not going to marry, leave his fortune, however small, to his children? Work was one of God's most blessed boons to Mankind. But the earning of a salary and the investing of money must have a meaning. Marriage was *sunnat*. Islam even advocated multiple marriages in a variety of situations. And of course, when he died, there would be his sons to wash and prepare his body, bury him, and pray for his soul. Aging and death were necessary concomitants of birth and life.

Thus, a debate between the merits and demerits of married life ranged in his mind, the words mingling their murmurings with those of the Pantai Tanjung Rhu waves and casuarinas.

At the end of his Pulau Langkawi stay, which he actually decided to cut short by three days, Pak Dollah had made up his mind. Despite the numerous burdens and problems marriage was likely to bring, it was a state of being much to be desired. He now wondered why he had waited so long to make such a decision.

During his visit to Din Keliang, the Siamese *bomoh,* Pak Dollah was no longer interested in checking if Fatimah binti Hussein or any other woman was in fact trying to charm him. He had come with other supplications — to seek a charm that would make him attractive to his future wife and to others, as well as to obtain an aphrodisiac. He knew the Siamese *bomoh* of Kedah were particularly skilled at preparing them from roots and herbs. In view of his present state of health, an aphrodisiac might come in handy, he thought.

When, after an absence of almost two weeks, a cheerful and virtually rejuvenated Pak Dollah returned to Kampung Dodol, he was welcomed with a *kenduri* and a *doa selamat*. Several of his colleagues from Sekolah Menengah Datuk Kaya had been invited.

On that occasion, Pak Dollah took the opportunity of announcing his momentous decision. When Pak Kadir suggested that the search for a suitable bride, once suspended, should now be resumed, Pak Dollah signalled that there was no need for such a search. He already had someone in mind. The only ones disappointed were the betel-munching matchmakers.

Two weeks later, Pak Dollah sent the traditional *hantaran* in twelve trays to the house of Fatimah binti Hussein, and in turn, received gifts from her parents. A month later, the *akad nikah* took place at Fatimah's house in Tasik Gelugor.

Pak Dollah was led in by Kampung Dodol *boria* and *kompang* groups. The female members of Pak Dollah's family, particularly the younger ones, insisted on a *bersanding*. Pak Dollah resisted the proposal, feeling shy at the thought of a forty-eight year old man sitting on a bersanding dais with a twenty-two year old girl. Finally, however, he succumbed to the persistent demands of his nieces, and a bersanding did take place. It is not known how many of those present that evening noticed Pak Dollah blushing.

That was several years ago. Fatimah bore Pak Dollah two children, a boy, now aged six, and a girl two years younger. Last year, at the age of fifty-five, the reluctant bridegroom married for the second time.

Pak Dollah had been attracted to Aminah binti Shamsudin, a widow transferred from Perak to Sekolah Menengah Datuk Kaya. Her husband, an army officer, had been killed in action by Communists at the Malaysian-Thai border. During the days following her arrival, Pak Dollah had developed a close, even intimate relationship with Aminah. Finally, though fully twenty years his junior, she had accepted his proposal. Pak Dollah reflected it as the will of God, for nothing happened unless God willed it.

The marriage took place soon after Pak Dollah's retirement. He had only recently celebrated his birthday with a kenduri and doa selamat. There were, however, some differences between this occasion and many of Pak Dollah's previous birthdays, particularly the forty-eighth. Some of the older members of his family, including Pak Kadir, were no longer with them. Pak Kadir had died three years before and lay buried in a grave adjacent to that of his father, Tuan Haji Abdul Karim, in the Perak Road Muslim Cemetery. For Pak Dollah's second marriage only a few guests had been invited. There had been no bersanding.

As the kadhi read the akad nikah, Pak Dollah wondered what else Fate had in store for him. How long more was he going to live? Was he going to be like his father, who married four times, or like his half-brother, who had acquire a third wife only a few months before his death? Well, reflected the piebald, bearded Pak Dollah, if it is God's Will, then nothing can stop it, for who can interfere with the workings of Providence?

This Pak Dollah had learnt as a little boy from his *ustaz;* this he had learnt from his father, Tuan Haji Abdul Karim; this he had learnt from his half-brother, the late Pak Kadir; this too he had learnt during his fifty-five years, and more particularly during the seven since his forty-eighth birthday.

THE OLD DICTATOR

The Old Dictator sat before a gigantic television screen, reputedly the largest in the city. The model had not yet been officially introduced into the country, but was expected to in the coming months. It had been presented to him when he had been kind enough to officiate at the opening of their new plant, by the well-known Mestibasi Corporation of Okinawa. This was but one of the many gifts the Datuk had received as a mark of gratitude from that particular company. And there were a whole lot of even more valuable gifts from other companies, mostly foreign, for the assistance he had rendered them in getting themselves set up in this country, notorious for delays and red-tapism, especially when he was in the Ministry of Foreign Investment. Naturally there were also numerous gifts, including cars and jewellery, for his wife, the Datin. This was only to be expected.

The Datuk was the chief executive of the administration in his own State. Due to his highly strict manner—those who hated his guts would say high-handed manner—of conducting business related to the administration of his State he had been nicknamed the Old Dictator. He was fully aware of this, but, of course, had to pretend that there was nothing of that sort, and, if indeed such a name had been given to him, it was all in good fun. What, after all, are nicknames but names that indicate admiration or jealousy, and one in his position had to be prepared for both types of situations—those giving rise to admiration as well as those giving rise to jealousy. It was all part of the game of politics. The Datuk had been in politics long enough to know this perfectly well. Personally, he was convinced that, like most of the leaders in this country, he was genial and generally well-loved. Like the most powerful of them, at times he too saw himself as being indispensable.

The Old Dictator sat before the huge television screen with the remote control in his right hand. He tried perhaps twenty or so channels in quick succession, now one channel, now another and then yet another. This he had done several times during the past hour or so, finding neither pleasure nor profit in watching any one of the channels on both the government and the private networks. The classical music channels seemed particularly jarring to his untrained ear; they had the tendency to send him off to sleep. As far as classical music was concerned he only vaguely knew two names—Beethoven and Mozart. He had heard that the Japanese used the music of Mozart to stimulate hair-growth. Amused, he brushed it aside as some kind of bad joke. That was the sum total of his knowledge about classical music. The news programmes no longer paid any attention to his activities. They had thus become irrelevant. The documentary channels spent too much time on animals and reptiles, while most of the film channels seemed to specialize in films that were not to his taste. The Western films had somehow become either too intellectual in content for him or too violent and noisy. As far as Malay films were concerned he preferred the old sentimental ones, particularly those featuring P. Ramlee. The heroines were sexy, the plots uncomplicated, and the music and songs, even though copied from Hindustani films, were memorable. But he could say without any doubt, that his preference was for Hindustani films, with their divine heroines, handsome heroes, lively music, songs, and dances, as well as everything else that one could possibly desire in a film.

Although not himself a particularly good singer or one endowed by Nature with a beautiful voice, he remembered how, in his youth, he used to go around trying to sing snatches of songs from *Sangam* or *Bobby*. His *Bhai* friends had told him that his pronunciation was not quite right, but did that really matter? After all he was singing merely for fun. How catchy and infectious the tunes of yesteryear had been!

In recent months, weeks and days the television programmes generally left a bad taste in his mouth, like the bitter medicine that he had had to swallow just a few minutes before. The Datin, accompanied by their pair of Indonesian maids, had brought in the whole trolley of pills, powders and mixtures, traditional and modern, as she did several times each day, making sure he took them on time. Never before in his life had he received so much personal attention from the Datin except during the days immediately following their marriage, memories of which now somehow seemed to lie buried in his remote past. The Datin had always had a great deal of leisure time, especially since she and the Datuk did not have children. She spent a lot of it traveling overseas, particularly back and forth between this country and Europe, shopping or idling with friends, particularly wives of other politicians. These days, with his illness, she devoted more time to him, carefully slotting him in between her other engagements.

The Datin had always been highly conscious of the latest fashions and trends, and he could not help but notice that, as usual, she was impeccably dressed in the latest fashions, and wore a great deal of jewellery, even during the hours that she spent at home. And to minister to his current needs, in addition to the Datin and the Indonesian maids, there was the whole gaggle of Malay *bomoh* and Chinese *sinseh* brought in by her to ensure his continued health and recovery. He could not but see, in all of these ministrations, something more than a pure and simple desire on the part of his first wife to be good to him. Somehow that did not fit in with what he knew of her character, having been married to her for over twenty years now. Fully twelve years younger to him, she seemed to have kept herself in very good shape, in spite of having put on some weight. Her childlessness had provided him with the excuse to marry not just one, but two more wives. She had not objected. Just reminded him that she was the senior of the three. And when he received the title of Datuk, naturally she became a Datin, a status she carried with considerable aplomb and relish.

The Old Dictator had just been discharged from the Gleneagles Medical Centre where he had stayed for two weeks of compulsory rest following a not-so-mild heart attack. He did not really mind the hospital stay. He was in the V.I.P. room, and was well taken care of. The nurses were pretty enough, coming and going from his room like angels all day long in their sparkling clean uniforms, and their ever-ready smiles. He had also received a fair number of visitors, including people he had not seen for a year or more. It had been a good change, in spite of the fact that, because of his attack, he was forced to devote at least some attention, with a degree of urgency, to problems he did not really wish to deal with at that point in his life, problems connected with his family and his assets. Some of the issues had now been settled, others were in the process of being resolved, and yet others would take a little more time. At least as far as his two younger wives and his children by those wives were concerned, he had done what he felt had to be done. They would not be left in any difficulties should anything happen to him. The pressure had been building up for some time and it had not been possible to delay the decisions any longer.

The Old Dictator looked a pathetic figure. His hair was almost totally gone except for the crescent-shaped slivers of grey just above his ears. Examining himself intently in the bathroom mirror just a little while ago, he could not even recognize himself without the wig or the crispy black Javanese *songkok* of the finest velvet, which regularly covered his head no matter whether he wore his specially-tailored Seville Row suits or his *baju Melayu* stitched by the best tailors in Singapore. He had seen his near-bald head perhaps thousands of times in the mirror, but his baldness had not struck him as strongly on those occasions as it did this evening. His head seemed to have a particularly strong sheen under the bathroom lamp. It was reflected by several strategically placed mirrors. He wondered why so many mirrors were needed in a single bathroom, almost as if the bathroom was in a five-star hotel. His face, generally fair, now distinctly pale, looked shapeless and ugly, his nose was one big blob, his eyes had dark rings around them. Seated in the chair in his sarong and T-shirt, his stomach protruding in the absence of the corset he regularly wore, he looked grossly overweight, despite the fact that he had in fact lost some weight due to illness, and now weighed only 195 pounds. The fact that he was short only served to accentuate his obesity. Totally transformed, he was in every possible way a pitiable figure, certainly appearing far older than his fifty-five years. He shut his eyes to close out the very image of himself, to close out his very being, but that proved quite a task.

The Old Dictator shifted his focus, visualized himself as he had been during his younger days when he had moved from a teaching job in a rural school to politics, beginning his political career at the district level and rising like a comet to the top ranks in his party hierarchy thanks both to good fortune and hard work. He focused more particularly on to where he stood during his heyday, not so long ago, before he lost the party election. Having reached the highest possible level in his own State as its chief executive, he was beginning to set his sights higher, actually at some Ministerial position at the Federal level. At the State level everything had been done to promote him as a young and capable leader. Experts from all over the world had been invited to do the public relations job; no expenses had been spared. To trim off pounds of his weight he had enrolled in the best gymnasia and health clubs. The official portraits displayed in government departments and in private homes, portraits taken more than twenty years earlier, showed him as a nearly-handsome personality, dressed in his bush-jacket, *baju Melayu* or Western suit. His tailors, his make-up artists, his hair-dressers, as well as his consultants in virtually every field of grooming and politics, together with his personal assistants, had tried to perpetuate in the minds of the *rakyat* that much-seen figure of a youngish Datuk that appeared on official portraits. The photographers, specially brought in from Australia, had undoubtedly done an outstanding job.

Seeing that he had reached such dizzy heights in such a short time, some people had begun to warn him that there were faint rumblings of anger, the beginnings of suspicion at the higher levels, that he should not behave as if he were a member of royalty, or that he was in any way special, even if he believed that he belonged to a Syed family.

On this there was no documented evidence. His South Indian grandfather had not used the title, neither had his father, but somewhere along the line, having discovered that he was born on a Thursday evening, a mysterious visitor from Andhra Pradesh, claiming to be a Sufi shaikh of sorts, had suggested that he add the word Syed to his name. This would undoubtedly enhance his standing in the world. He immediately recognized that was a brilliant idea, particularly since he was just then entering the complicated world of politics. And so he had changed his name by deed poll, got his identity card replaced, and claimed that in fact he had been a Syed all along, even though his birth certificate provided no evidence of it. As a matter of precaution, instead of spelling the new honorific in its traditional style as S-y-e-d, or S-a-y-y-i-d in the South Indian fashion, he spelled it as S-a-i-d, thus making it less conspicuous. He was convinced that this change in name and identity had certainly been one of the factors behind his meteoric rise in the world of local politics. But Allah knows best.

But the figure or rather image that he had created for himself at great cost and trouble that was the figure he hoped would remain in the minds of the *rakyat* in his State, and perhaps eventually the *rakyat* of the country. He had expected to remain in politics, and in some position of power, for the rest of his days. He recalled the names of a number of past politicians who had been appointed Governors in various States of the country. Why should such an eventuality be altogether ruled out in his case? He knew that everyone had to go one day that even the most famous would one day become obscure. That was the Will of Allah. All the same he wanted, at all costs, to leave a pleasant image in the minds of at least a generation or two of his fellow citizens. A personal image and not just a name through the numerous resorts and monuments that he had built in his State and particularly in its capital, Kuala Mas. He was certain that some of these places and monuments would eventually be named in his honour. Given the way things inevitably went, there was, of course, always the possibility that some leader in the decades following him would once again, as he himself had done, replace these names to reflect a new reality, even possibly change the State's capital. Reasons could always be found.

The photographs had been taken with just such an idea—that of projecting an image of a youthful and dynamic leader. The appearances on television had in every possible way maintained that image. Even the specially commissioned official biographies and "autobiographies" (written for him by others) reflected the greatness and benevolence of the Old Dictator. He was depicted in the glossy pages as a smiling leader, meting out generous gifts in orphanages or old folks' homes during festivals, giving fiery speeches attacking other nations, including even the world's greatest powers that dared to criticize this country's political system, supposedly, according to their standards, undemocratic, as if there was only one kind of democracy in the world—their kind. He had enjoyed every moment of the power and the glory, every minute in the limelight.

And then, all of a sudden there had come the great fall. By merely a difference of 89 votes he had been removed. The shock was too great for him to bear; he was certain there had been a conspiracy to remove him. And as if on cue, promptly he had had a heart attack. Despite the best of medical care and attention throughout the past few years, his cholesterol level had reached dangerous levels. The images of his past successes that kept flashing on the screen of his mind had only served to heighten his insomnia. He felt depressed, he felt giddy. He had to be hospitalized for a rest and for further medical tests. And it was under these circumstances, while he was in hospital, that the second attack had come. He wondered what would have happened if the attack had, by chance, come when he was at home, rather than in the Gleneagles Medical Centre. Utter care had to be taken for there could be a recurrence, and he had been warned that the next attack could prove to be fatal. He needed prolonged rest in hospital, and later on at home. The extended hospital stay had had a devastating effect upon his body and spirit. Each night, dreaming of his days of glory, days that were never to return, he would feel utterly helpless.

The poignancy of the situation came to the Datuk with a shock when the realized that many of those who used to huddle around him day and night now no longer even came to see him. On the night he was admitted into the hospital, there had been several dozen people, apart from his family. But the number kept declining by the day, and by the time he was discharged there was hardly anyone.

He had returned to his bungalow with the Datin, their driver, and his former political secretary. There was no one else. Perhaps it was a good thing. He did not want to be seen in the condition in which he was at that time. It would have been bad for his image.

Promptly, the Datin had called the whole circle of his friends and former officials as well as members of his political party to inform them that the Datuk was now resting at home, and that he would be happy to receive visitors, although not in large numbers, during reasonable hours; she even encouraged several of them to make the visit. The doctors had suggested that some company would be good for the Datuk, as long as precautions were taken not to over-strain him.

Since then the Datuk had looked forward to his friends' visits, but the number of visitors had been but a trickle. He was much disillusioned. There was a sense of emptiness in him as he sat before the huge television screen during the daylight hours and the early hours of the night, watching now one, now another programme, reading and re-reading the day's newspapers, as well as the one serious book that he had been advised, during his younger days as an upcoming politician, to read with great diligence. This was Machiavelli's *The Prince*. He had never been a great reader. Neither did he have the time for reading nor did he feel it necessary to read. What was the point of reading, when one was already successful, when even one's speeches were written by someone else? Before actually reading a speech in public, all one had to do, if one had the time and inclination, was to browse through it, to check for any difficult words, change them into simpler ones, master the manner in which they were to be pronounced, and determine where emphases were needed. In time even these things became unnecessary as his Secretaries got used to the level of the Datuk's linguistic abilities as well as his particular manner of reading from prepared texts. After that, it had all become routine. The prepared speech would be presented to him, and he would store it in the inner pocket of his coat. At the appropriate moment, he would take it out with a flourish, perch his reading glasses on his nose, and read in a suitable style, with appropriate emotion and intensity, punctuating the speech with appropriate flourishes of his right hand. Now he knew that there would be no more speeches ever again; his career as a leader and a politician was dead. The Machiavelli volume still lay on the side-table, with his gold-rimmed reading glasses in a fancy case, but now he saw the futility of reading even *The Prince*. He did not remember having gone through the volume even once.

The Datin informed him that his lawyers were at hand. He had earlier in the day made arrangements to see them. Still dressed in a sarung, he put on a *baju Melayu*, placed his *songkok* on his head to cover his bald patch, and prepared himself for the final step in his diminution. The time had come for him to give instructions regarding his personal assets. He knew for a certainty that with his position now so drastically changed, there would come a time when everything he owned would be scrutinized, when much of it would be taken away from him. The Inland Revenue Department had been sending him reminders. For several years he did not even realize that such a department existed. Very strong rumours had begun to circulate in recent months that the Anti-Corruption Agency was getting extremely interested in him. Officers from the agency had been asking questions from several persons closely associated with him. This he had gathered from a few of his once close friends who still maintained links with him. Now, of course, given the twist in the events, they were cautious. They apologized for not wishing to be seen with him. Instead of coming in for personal discussions or even talking over the telephone, they sent brief notes through mutual friends or through their drivers.

Yet again, the Datin was getting anxious. What if there was another heart attack, a more serious one? She hesitated to use the word "final". Best to get some of the more valuable assets transferred to her name, as well as to the names of her nominees. Best that this was done before the Datuk's other relatives came in, as if from nowhere, to stake their claims. Once this was done, her husband could, for all she cared, very well prepare for the next stroke, succumb to it when it came.

The lawyers came in with certain relevant documents; these were carefully scrutinized. Those that could not be made available in the short time given would be brought in at some other time. It became clear to the Old Dictator that matters could not be settled that easily, that a considerable amount of time was needed, particularly to deal with the assets abroad, including those in Australia, the United Kingdom and in Swiss banks. It could not all be done from his sick-bed. The Datuk himself would have to travel quite a bit to give his personal attention to certain matters. At the present time he was in no position to undertake strenuous journeys.

During the several following days the lawyers kept coming in, and each visit saw several hours of discussions. During this time, the Datin herself became by turn increasingly apprehensive and disappointed. From her point of view, everything had to be done urgently. The ACA might be descending upon the Datuk at any time, and it was impossible to predict how soon the next heart attack would come. What would happen to all those assets, particularly the overseas ones, in the event that the Datuk suddenly passed away? It was clear that the lawyers could not provide straightforward answers. Things were much more complicated than she or the Old Dictator had anticipated.

Meanwhile, during all of these strenuous and serious discussions, the Datuk felt a wide range of contrary emotions. Ultimately, little by little, he came to the realisation that there was no way in which he could possibly enjoy his assets, even though he had gone through thick and thin to collect all the wealth, through honest, dishonest and often highly questionable means. If at all, his three wives, his children and grandchildren would be those who would stand to gain, provided there were no complications, after the ACA had come and gone, after the taxes had been paid, after all debts and liabilities had been cleared. It was obvious that, no matter how things went, he would have to part with a good percentage of his wealth. And, as far as he himself was personally concerned he could see very little to comfort him. He was really not in any position to enjoy his wealth. Yes, that was the bottom line.

His mind, all of a sudden crystal clear, now began to momentarily ignore the assets, whose actual value he himself was not sure off, hidden somewhere in the muddle of accounts. He wondered if it would really matter if they-- his wives and children, as well as any of his other relatives, if indeed they had any claims—if they did not receive anything. And his grandchildren or their children, and their children after that? They were yet to be born. He did not see how he could be held responsible for their welfare since he would have made his exit from this world stage by the time they made their entrance. All material wealth seemed suddenly to become meaningless. It dawned upon him that his pursuit of power and posterity was no more than a sort of means for self-satisfaction, a challenge to prove something to himself, and perhaps to others. Nothing more. *That* he had already achieved, having lived an interesting, and in his own terms, meaningful, life. Beyond that did anything matter at all? He could not, like the Chinese, send millions of dollars in Hell Bank notes to the next world to open their accounts there by just burning bundles of paper. That had always intrigued him--the fact that the invisible bankers of the next world would be willing to accept all the fake "currency" printed on cheap paper, purchased for a song. He would certainly be willing, he thought, to send some of his real currency to the next world if, indeed, this country's currency or the currency of any other country on earth—the US dollar or the British pound, for instance, was legal tender in the next world. The idea amused him.

His lawyers had left. There would be further meetings and discussions in the coming days. For now he was all alone in the lounge, slouched in his black leather seat. What was he to do now, at this stage of his precarious existence?

He narrowed down his immediate problems to two: the ACA and the next heart attack. He began to wonder what it would be like to spend the rest of his years in prison following the undoubtedly sensational news of his arrest and trial. Also, he wondered what it would be like to come face to face with the pair of fearsome questioning angels, Munkir and Nakir, given the fact that he had acquired virtually no knowledge of even the rudimentary teachings of his religion. He was prepared for neither prison nor the trial of the grave. He shuddered at both prospects, momentarily pushed them aside. And what about his present situation? He was thoughtful for a while, reflective. Of a sudden he came to a momentous possibility. He would instruct his lawyers to negotiate with the Inland Revenue Department as well as with the Anti-Corruption Agency, ask them to work out a compromise settlement.

More importantly, he would dole out huge sums of money to charitable organizations, making sure these events got full media coverage, appearing in the national newspapers as headlines and on to the television screens. In the coming days he himself would personally appear at Press conferences, dressed immaculately as in his heyday, in his *baju Melayu*, his wig, his Indonesian *songkok* of the finest black velvet, to make those heroic announcements of his magnanimity.

A strange mood came over him, a mood of inexplicable bravado.
He called in one of his Indonesian maids, asked her to get his driver
to buy the best mutton *beriyani* from Bilal's and to get him a bottle
of brandy for dinner from his locked wooden cabinet. It had been
years since his last glass of brandy, years since his bar at home had
been opened. He switched on his compact disc player, put it into
repeat mode, and inserted a disc, fast-forwarded to a particular
piece. The video-clip showed a scene from *Sangam*, a scene indelibly
imprinted on the memory of the Old Dictator. .

> *Tere man ki Ganga, aur mere man ki Jamna ka*
> *Bol Radha bol, sangam ho ga keh nahin.*

He had never found out the precise meanings of the words.
Years and years ago he had been given a loose translation by one of
his friends, a Muslim officer at the Indian High Commission. The
song touched upon the coming together of the two great rivers, the
Ganges and the Jamuna (on which stood the Taj Mahal), serving as
a symbol for the seemingly impossible union of the lovers. The scene
was played by Raj Kapoor and Vyjayanthimala. In his present state
the Datuk saw this as having a greater meaning than hitherto already
given to him--as the fusion of this world and the next.

Surprised at his own ingenuity, the Old Dictator rose from his
black leather seat and began to sway from side to side in a waltz,
began to gyrate, simultaneously echoing, over and over again, the
words of the song, in Hindustani, in consonance with the singers.
Reaching a state of near ecstasy he laughed, laughed louder and
louder. A few minutes later the Datin rushed in, with the Indonesian
maids in tow, switched off the video compact disc player.

> *Hey Abang! Apa dah jadi ini? Dah gila kah?* [1]

---

[1]   Hey Husband, what is the matter with you? Have you gone crazy?

SUJJAN SINGH

The morning traffic on Chulia Street was beginning to build up, the vehicles turning sharply into the narrow street from the ferry terminal and then rushing towards Penang Road, their speed dampened only by the two sets of traffic lights at the Beach Street and Pitt Street junctions. The advancing day would not only bring in greater volumes of traffic and noise, but also hot storms of street-dust with the thumping passage of each set of heavy wheels.

Chulia Street had been a popular, and in some ways unavoidable, thoroughfare since the very founding of Georgetown. Undoubtedly much had changed since that fateful day in 1786 that brought the British, and with them the Indians, the Chinese and the Eurasians to Penang. Eventually the Indians and Chinese, in particular, were to fan out into other parts of the Malay peninsula, and to be joined by members of other communities as well. But even now Chulia Street, as well as the numerous narrow streets and alleys in its vicinity, in the area marked out by the British for Penang's first urban settlement, retained their old-world charm, a strange mixture of India with all its complexities, of China and of Great Britain. Conspicuous too was the imprint of many lesser cultures.

Time seemed to have frozen in Chulia Street as in much of Georgetown. Time had brought independence and time too had seen the collapse of the British empire and Great Britain inexorably decline into a nation that remained great only in name.

Murli's shop in the Indian section of Chulia Street near the Nagore memorial shrine, the section in which businesses owned by Sindhi, Gujerati and Punjabi merchants as well as by Tamil Muslims were prominent, had been open for only a few minutes. The beige collapsible metal shutters had been pushed aside. The dark-green bamboo-strip blinds, the name Makhanlal & Sons, Textiles and General Merchants, prominent on them in bold red with a black shadow, had been lowered to prevent the invasion of the morning interior by the warm and spreading sunlight. The address and other details appeared in smaller letters on the blinds, while at the very top was emblazoned, in solid black, the information "Established 1935", clear and unmistakable evidence, for the notice of all passersby that the business had been operating for nearly half a century. The space on the lower half of the blinds was taken up by large reproductions of multi-coloured *kain pelikat* labels—Chop Gadjah and Chop Sauh, strategically placed on both sides of the cut-out centre section which allowed for entrance into the premises, the entrance itself covered by a plain, dark blue curtain.

Makhanlal & Sons' set of blinds resembled many on Chulia Street, only differing in colour and the labels indentifying the sponsoring *sarung* manufacturers and suppliers, most of whom had their principal offices in faraway Madras. These blinds remain, to this day, an ubiquitous feature of Penang's "little India".

Subramaniam, the *thamby*, aged perhaps twenty-two, his forehead marked with stripes of burnt ash, an indication that he had been to the morning *pooja*, was sprinkling water on the *kaki lima*, the five-foot path, after having swept it clean. The sprinkling of water, a common practice amongst Little India shopkeepers, apart from creating a feeling of coolness, served to prevent dust from flying into the premises.

The heady aroma of fresh jasmines mixed with that of incense sticks lighted each morning in Murli's shop before gaudy-looking portraits of the blue-skinned Lord Krishna in his pose as flute-player, of Sai Baba and the smiling late *Seth* Makhanlalji, still hung thick in the air mixed with benzoin smoke rising langurously but no longer in full intensity, from a clay censer placed under a table.

The shop had been swept clean and Murli himself was just beginning to arrange the rolls of cloth in one of his showcases when Sujjan Singh appeared.

"*Namaste*, Murliji. Good morning."

Sujjan Singh was dressed, as usual, in white *kurta* and *churidhar* pants. That morning he wore a reddish-orange turban which, to Murli, seemed somewhat carelessly tied, and a pair of upturned, carved leather *chappal*. Sujjan Singh was of medium build, perhaps five feet six inches in height, and had a paunch. He raised his hands in *anjali* gesture, his black umbrella dangling precariously from his left arm together with a not-too-clean Shakti Flour Mills canvas bag. His long, grey beard, unkempt, gave him the appearance of a holy man, a *sadhu*. And with Sujjan Singh's entrance, a new but yet familiar odour wafted into the interior of Makhanlal & Sons, to mingle with diverse others.

Sujjan Singh usually greeted persons younger to him in English. When greeting Sikh elders or those of his own age he used the Punjabi greeting *Sat Sri Akal*. For non-Sikhs it was *Namasteji*, and occasionally, half-jocularly, he would address his Muslim friends with *Assalaamu alaikum*. Sujjan Singh had acquired the English language during his younger days in school and, following that, during the many years of loyal service in the Postal Department of Malaya's British Administration.

Sujjan Singh had come to Malaya in his childhood with his parents, Pritam Singh and Pyar Kaur, from his father's native village in the Punjab not far from Jullundur. Pritam had from his arrival in Malaya, been a milk-vendor. Additionally, he had set himself up as a money-lender, to supplement his income, carrying on this second occupation without any proper license. Pritam Singh's one hope was that his five children, and especially his sons, Tara Singh and Sujjan Singh, would have better lives than he himself had had. He made sure they went to school. Both Tara Singh and Sujjan Singh entered the same class on the same day in the very same school in which Sujjan Singh had studied; the medium of instruction was the English language. Tara Singh was already twelve years old while Sujjan was two years younger. Tara Singh lost interest in studying and dropped out of school, much to his father's disappointment, after four years. He assisted his father in the milk-vending business and eventually set up a small stall in the Piccadilly bazaar to sell textiles. Sujjan Singh completed his primary education as well as three years at the secondary level. Not many months after his education thus came to an end, Pritam Singh packed both his sons off to India to be married. The brides-to-be were two nieces of Kartar Kaur. Neither Tara Singh nor Sujjan Singh had met their brides before the marriage. While Tara Singh decided to stay a little longer in Jullundur, Sujjan Singh decided that he should return to Malaya as soon as possible following the marriage. As it happened in fact, Tara Singh stayed on in the Punjab for more than a year, before returning to Penang with his wife and a baby boy. It was at this point that Tara Singh set up his textiles business in the bazaar.

Sujjan Singh and his bride Kartar Kaur made a brief visit to the Golden temple in Amritsar before proceeding on to Delhi and then took the train to Calcutta to embark a Penang-bound ship. Sujjan Singh had been away from Penang almost exactly two months. The marriage of Sujjan Singh and Kartar Kaur was blessed with four children—two sons and two daughters, but one of the girls died in infancy. Tara Singh and his wife, on the other hand, had six children—four sons and two daughters.

Within three months of his return to Malaya, Sujjan Singh joined the Postal Department, serving in several different towns, and rising over the years from the position of postman to postmaster. All through this period, following the example of his father, Sujjan Singh also operated as an unlicensed money lender, giving out small amounts, usually not exceeding two hundred Malaysian ringgit, mainly to the Tamil workers in the Postal Department. After his retirement, Sujjan Singh decided to devote greater attention to his money-lending business and, on the whole, did reasonably well although, inevitably, there were some bad debts. All in all he had been able to live very comfortably, send money to his native Punjab to buy some property at the suggestion of his late father and the assistance of his uncles and cousins.

Sujjan Singh was proud of his service to the British, in recognition of which he had received a medal from the last British Governor of the Straits Settlements. He was equally proud of his ability to handle the language of the British with a facility rare amongst those of his generation. Although not particularly learned, he was in total agreement with the many Indian scholars who claimed that English, or rather *Angrezi*, was an Indian language. After all there were countless millions of speakers of English in India, more than in the Unite Kingdom or in any other country. From his own reading of popular magazines, especially the *Illustrated Weekly of India*, he knew that the Indians had managed to produce outstanding personalities in almost every field in which English had to be used, including even literature or *adab*. He noted with satisfaction that some of the

most outstanding literary figures were Punjabis—Rajinder Singh
Bedi, Sa'adat Hassan Manto, Amrita Pritam and Khushwant Singh.

In school Sujjan Singh had been exposed to some British
literature. He particularly liked English poetry and knew Shakespeare
in passing from Lamb's *Tales from Shakespeare*. On several occasions
he tried reading *The Merchant of Venice*, his favourite Shakespearean
story, in its original, but found it too long; and Shakespeare's
language, even though it was English, was certainly way beyond
him. He was proud of his now dirty and dog-eared volume of the
play, which he treasured. But he knew the plot of *The Merchant
of Venice* through and through. He was particularly fascinated
with the character of Shylock. Sujjan Singh somehow always felt
that Shakespeare had been thoroughly biased in his delineation of
Shylock. Of course, as a money-lender himself Sujjan Singh could
sympathize with Brabantio, but that was another issue. Portia, he
thought, was a marvelously drawn character. As the years passed, he
had increasingly given up serious reading even in Urdu and Punjabi,
languages that he had learnt respectively from his father and the
granthi of the Sikh Temple. Right now his own favourite reading
was the *Guru Granth Sahib* and the immortal story of *Heer Ranjha*
as told by Waris Shah, the great mystic poet of the Punjab. This
immortal classic Sujjan had read over and over again, and he had
heard the recordings of its songs countless times, his eyes brimming
with tears, a sign of the stirrings in his Punjabi soul.

Sujjan Singh certainly admired both the English language and
the literature written in it; after all English *was* undeniably an Indian
language. Yes, the Indians were proud of their *Angrezi,* and they used
it with a flourish lacking even among the British.

As far as the Britishers themselves were concerned, Sujjan Singh's
attitudes were ambivalent. While he enjoyed his service with them,
and was thankful for much that he had learnt from them, as well

as for his continuing monthly pension of ringgit 356.30, when it came to politics, he had not a single kind word for them, the *"salay Angrez log"*, as he called them. He was particularly upset with the manner in which the British had ruined the many kingdoms that dotted the ancient and beautiful land of Hindustan like jewels in a crown. And undeniably the greatest of the jewels was Punjab. The Jallianwala Bagh massacre was a particularly serious blot on the British Raj. According to Sujjan Singh's interpretation of Indian history, the British had deliberately ruined Indian kingdoms, set the Hindus against the Musalmans and the Sikhs mercilessly in between to be slaughtered by both. It was a ploy to ensure that they and their Western allies, particularly Amrika, could continue to sell their weapons for generations to come. *"The salay Angrez log"*, he cursed, unheard by anyone. It went without saying that the Indians themselves were to blame. It was a well-known fact that many of them, princes and paupers alike, to their utter and permanent disgrace, were lackeys of the British, in league with them. They should have been torn to bits and thrown to the dogs.

"Can anyone believe that the Indians were so stupid—helping the *salay gore log* to kill their own countrymen? Helping the bloody foreigners to conquer their own ancient land? What did they get in return?" Sujjan Singh would ask passionately, his anger almost uncontrollable.

He had his answers to that question; but they required in their utterance the inclusion of the choicest of vulgar words in his more than ample Punjabi vocabulary. And so he seldom uttered them, except in the right company. Sujjan Singh's favourite topic was the first Indian War of Independence, described in British history books to this day as the "Indian mutiny".

"Mutiny, my foot," Sujjan Singh would respond, his *Angrezi* language coloured with a full dose of his Punjabi passion each time the topic was mentioned. His blood boiled and he could not prevent himself using filthy words to describe the colonial masters. In the company of refined hearers he would habitually apologize when such profanities issued uncontrollably from his lips. He did not wish to hurt their sensibilities. The vulgarities, of course, became understandably coarser when he spoke in his native tongue.

Sujjan Singh lamented the tragic loss of millions of lives during the months preceding the bloody partition of Hindustan in August 1947--Hindus, Muslims and Sikhs alike, some closely related to his family--when at last the British were forced out. He always felt that if partition of the sub-continent was necessary at all, then the British should have provided for the creation of Khalistan, a Sikh homeland. After all if the Hindus could have their Hindustan—to him India was an artificial, meaningless and even idiotic name for the country—and the Pakistanis their Pakistan, was it really that unthinkable that the Sikhs should have been given their Khalistan? Had the British had the sense and the foresight to create Khalistan, they would certainly have been less hateful in his eyes, his vulgarities would have been rendered superfluous, and he may even have been able to express full admiration for their diplomacy. Still, he was proud of his *Angrezi*, and would avail himself with enthusiasm of every available opportunity to use it.

"Are *Bhai*, where would the Indians be," he was fond of saying, "if they did not have their *Angrezi*? You call Hindi a language? Do you think Hindi could have united the Indians with their God-alone-knows how many different races, colours, religions and tongues? And don't forget, they also have their caste system, as if life was not problematic enough without it. Just leave it to the Indians, and they will complicate everything."

Murli responded to Sujjan Singh's greeting.

"Namaste, Chachaji."

Although Sujjan Singh was by far the older of the two, being in fact a close friend of Seth Makhanlalji, Murli's father, he habitually took the initiative of greeting Murli first, even habitually using the honorific -*ji* after his name.

This had always been the case between Seth Makhanlalji and Sujjan Singh, for Sujjan Singh had a high degree of regard for the late Makhanlal. Not only was Makhanlal senior in terms of age, he also had the important advantage of *izzat* in the Malaysian Indian community, particularly among the influential Sindhi, Gujerati and Punjabi merchants. Sujjan Singh was well aware of the fact that, to a great extent, there is a correspondence between a person's wealth and the degree of respect his community accorded him. It is well known that in most cases, though not particularly in the case of the late Seth Makhanlalji, wealth served as a means of purchasing status, titles, and so on in this country. Here the feudal mentality had not altogether been given up. The level of education one attained or other qualifications one had did not really count. In fact many less than mediocre people had gone very far. It was whom one knew that mattered, and the wealthier one was the more the opportunities became available to further one-self. This seemed to him to be the case, particularly with those who had entered politics, for Sujjan Singh was at one time an avid reader of English language newspapers and magazines, both Malaysian and Indian. In the popular magazines, there were always in-depth stories as well as a variety of scandals, including those concerning prominent new-rich businessmen or politicians who were involved with teenage girls, even with upcoming film stars. Outside the realm of politics, such as in social relations among the Indians, when there wasn't wealth then other criteria became applicable--such as whether one was a doctor, lawyer or engineer. This Sujjan Singh had observed through all the years of his life.

In Seth Makhanlalji Sujjan Singh saw an example of someone genuinely meriting respect. He had wealth, but more importantly, he had a generous, friendly disposition. He was an important pillar of Penang's Indian community, unstintingly supportive of its activities. Sujjan Singh's admiration for Seth Makhanlalji was not misplaced. He was absolutely certain of that. With the passing of Seth Makhanlalji, the respect he had for the late *seth* was transferred to Murli. This was only appropriate. In Sujjan Singh's thinking, age or seniority did not really matter. He enjoyed his humility.

Apart from all this, of course, Sujjan did have an instinctive liking for Murli as well as for Murli's younger Bansilal. Bansilal was completing his medical studies in Chandigarh University. Sujjan Singh had for several years even entertained fond hopes of making Bansilal his son-in-law; but now that Seth Makhanlalji had passed away, that subject had not been broached. Sujjan was at a loss as to how it could be raised, if at all, with Murli. His resolve, however, remained as strong as ever, and any connection with the family of Seth Makhanlalji would not only give his daughter, Jaswant Kaur, a good husband and a desirable home, it would also assure Sujjan himself of greater *izzat* in the community. He had considered the possibility, when the time came, of seeking the assistance of someone close to Seth Makhanlal's family to pursue the subject. There were several such persons in the Penang business community whose assistance he could call upon when the time came. There was, of course, the problem of religious differences—Seth Makhanlal's family was fairly orthodox Hindus. Although he was aware that his own Sikh *biradari* would not take any such alliance sympathetically, he was certain that the problem could be overcome. After all both the families were Punjabis and in fact even originated in the same district in the native land. And, come to think of it, was there really a big difference between Hindus and Sikhs? The Sikhs had taken over many Hindu traditions and customs leaving out idol worship, and modifying some of the beliefs only slightly. These combined with elements similarly borrowed from the Muslims, particularly the Sufis, gave rise to Sikhism. The Sikh scriptures clearly demonstrated these borrowings. Why even one of the names that the Sikhs gave God was Allah, the very name used by Muslims. Nevertheless, although basically, the cultures of the Punjabis, whether they were Hindus, Muslims or Sikhs, were the same, major differences in the religions of the Muslims and the Sikhs made marriages between these communities unthinkable. The traditional hatred the Sikhs had developed for the Muslims as a result of political developments in India during the late Mughal Empire had not been altogether forgotten, and a Sikh who became a Muslim would immediately be considered an outcaste. With the Hindus, however, it was different. Sujjan Singh knew of many inter-marriages between Hindus and Sikhs in Malaysia. Surely there was nothing wrong with that, as long as the Hindus were from north India, and especially if they were Punjabis, he quickly added in his own mind. He could not stand the thought of any of his children marrying Tamils or Chinese. He recoiled even more at the thought that they would get involved with Malays and thus have to become Muslims, according to the *syariah* law. Such an event, should it transpire in his family, would surely be the death of him, he knew. He would have nowhere to hide his face. Sujjan Singh felt that it was only a question of approach now. It would have been easier to approach Seth Makhanlalji than to approach Murli. He would not have been offended even if there had been a rebuff from the Sethji.

Sujjan Singh had often mulled over these thoughts. At times he sensed a degree of fear in himself on three possible accounts. Firstly, the Sethji's family was wealthy and would obviously seek alliances with others of their standing. Secondly, he could not anticipate how

Murli, Murli's mother, and other members of the Makhanlal family would react to the differences in religion between their family and his own, should he at any time build up enough courage to approach them. They may not necessarily see things from his own perspective. And thirdly, there was the concern of how his own community would react. Although he did not himself have many Sikh friends, he still had to maintain links with his *biradari*, particularly when it came to *gurdwara* matters and matters related to birth, marriage and death. In such situations it was vital to have a support system upon which one could depend. He did not wish to be ostracized by the Sikhs.

Each time he reflected upon these issues Sujjan Singh's head reeled. Each time a decision was postponed. After all, he reflected, Jaswant Kaur was only touching seventeen. He could wait a year or two, and by that time the whole scenario might have changed. He decided, therefore, for the umpteenth time, to leave the whole matter in God's hands.

Murli looked at his watch and also at the wall-clock. Despite a difference of about five minutes in the two timekeepers, there was no mistake as far as the time of day was concerned. It was a quarter to nine according to his watch and about twenty minutes to nine if his wall clock was to be believed. Mohini, his salesgirl had not yet reported for work, and she was the very symbol of punctuality, arriving each morning on the dot at nine.

Sujjan Singh sensed the surprise in Murli.

"I am a little early today", he said.

Murli mused. Sujjan Singh was in fact more than eight hours early, considering that each day he made his entry into the premises of Makhanlal & Sons, Textiles and General Merchants at about five o'clock in the evening. Sujjan Singh's tone was grave this morning. Murli sensed that something unusual had brought Sujjan Singh this early to his shop. Sujjan Singh was a regular visitor, having been coming to the shop for years now. Sujjan Singh and Seth Makhanlal had been close friends, although the Sethji was the senior of the two by about ten years. It was their custom to meet in the Sethji's shop before proceeding for tea at Krishna's Place, a South Indian tea shop, no bigger or cleaner than a stall, at the junction of Market Street and Queen Street. Krishna's Place had a reputation for good snacks.

"The best *masala tosai* in town." Seth Makhanlal used to say. He also had high praise for their tea, especially if it was made with fresh milk and was *kurang manis*. Although the *teh tarik* at the restaurant was also good, Seth Makhanlalji avoided it due to high content of sugar. But in Seth Makhanlalji's view no one could question the quality of the *tosai* at Krishna's.

"Nothing beats their *uppama*," Sujjan Singh was fond of teasing his friend.

Sujjan Singh had a particular predilection towards the *uppama* at Krishna's. The Sethji, on the other hand, eschewed *uppama*. "Too oily for me", he would say. "And you too should take care of your health, Sujjan *Bhai*. After all you are not growing any younger."

The Sethji, who was overweight according to his doctor, had both high blood pressure and diabetes; Dr Ananda Moorthy had warned him to severely restrict his diet. Seth Makhanlal obeyed his dictates as best as he could; on the whole he remained quite healthy until his last days, and death, when it came on a December evening three years before, was brought about by heart failure. Sujjan Singh's heart was broken. For several weeks he became inconsolable at the loss of his dear friend who had the remarkable ability to blur the boundaries between rich and poor. Over the days, weeks, months and years, although he had become reconciled to Makhanlalji's death, he still felt the Seth's strong presence in the premises of Makhanlal & Sons.

Sujjan Singh had continued to visit Murli almost without fail following Seth Makhanlalji's death. The routine of the visit to Krishna's was discontinued. Instead, tea and *uppama* were sent for, and Sujjan Singh had his evening snack in Murli's air-conditioned office. Murli himself would have a cup of *teh tarik*, just to keep Sujjan Singh company.

Under the circumstances Sujjan Singh's appearance this early in the day was a cause for some concern. Murli, however, did not wish to embarrass Sujjan Singh by seeking explanations for the change in routine. He felt certain that Sujjan Singh would, in due course, venture them himself.

"Shall I send for some snacks?" Murli asked.

"Perhaps just some tea. Nothing else, thank you."

Maniam was promptly sent to order two cups of tea, while Murli guided Sujjan into his office.

"Would you mind switching off the air-conditioner, Murli *beta*?" Sujjan Singh requested. "The morning is still cool. I hope you don't mind."

"Oh, that's alright, Chachaji."

Murli obliged by switching off the air-conditioner; he switched on the ceiling fan instead. The tea came and the two of them sat in the office. Murli noticed that Mohini had just come in. Getting leave from Sujjan, he went out to give her some instructions.

"I hope everything is alright, uncle. You don't look too cheerful this morning," he said, rejoining Sujjan Singh.

He felt genuine concern for Sujjan Singh, whom he had known since his childhood. On the whole although he had seen Sujjan grow older over the years, Murli noticed that he had not aged visibly. Sujjan Singh had just completed his fifty-seventh year, having retired from the Postal Services department two years before.

"Oh, I'm alright, alright. Nothing wrong with me, Murli beta. Nothing I . . . I just had a restless night; had to come in as soon as possible to see you. I hope you don't mind. . ."

"No, not at all, not at all."

There was momentary silence between the two men. Sujjan Singh, putting some snuff into his nostrils, broke the silence with a loud sneeze. He began to speak slowly, in a manner that Murli had never before seen in Sujjan Singh.

"You see, when I went home yesterday evening, I found a letter from Ranjit waiting for me." Sujjan Singh, reaching for the side-pocket on his *kurta*, produced an aerogramme which had been folded into two. It had obviously been folded and unfolded several times.

Ranjit, Sujjan Singh's son, was studying medicine in India. Murli and Ranjit, two years his senior, had had been school-mates. Ranjit had not been able to get through his Higher School Certificate examination, and so, ineligible for a place in a local university, he had been sent off to a college not far from Madras to do his pre-medical studies with the expectation that he would continue to study for a degree in medicine. That was almost ten years ago, and Ranjit Singh was still nowhere near to completing his studies. As far as Murli knew, Ranjit had failed virtually every year, and there was only an extremely slim possibility that he would ever return to Malaysia a qualified doctor.

"You can read it yourself." Sujjan Singh extended the aerogramme towards Murli. "There's nothing confidential in it. Besides you are like a son to me. Go on, take it."

Murli reluctantly took the letter from Sujjan Singh. Written in English, it began with the usual opening greetings and humble apologies for not writing for the past several months. Ranjit went on to indicate that he had decided to give up his medical studies; he had no interest in medicine. He expressed his desire to enter the Indian film industry as an actor, and hoped that his father would not be too upset at his new plans. He had, in fact, already started visiting various studios in the Madras area to make inquiries for possible openings, even for minor roles. If nothing worked out in Madras, he wrote, he would move to Bombay to try his luck there.

Murli folded the letter slowly; without saying a word, handed it back to Sujjan Singh. Both men sat as if in a state of trance, each hesitant to make the first statement, each not knowing how to proceed. Murli could sense the old man's anguish; internally he was both amused as well disturbed at Ranjit's audacity, shocked at his wild scheme. He avoided looking directly at Sujjan Singh's face. Sujjan Singh closed his eyes, and placed both his hands on his face for a few seconds, and then removed his hands with a sigh. His hands now folded on his lap, Sujjan Singh lowered his head, shaking it from side to side in obvious agony.

The ringing of the telephone provided Murli with a timely break. It was a call from one of his suppliers in Singapore, inquiring about payment for some overdue bills. Not wanting Sujjan Singh to get the impression that he had difficulty making payments on time, Murli avoided prolonging the conversation. He promised his distant caller that he was at a meeting and that he would look into the matter as soon as possible.

"Well, what do you think?" Sujjan Singh tried to steer Murli's attention to the letter.

"I can understand your disappointment, Chachaji. But what can I say? Perhaps he is thinking of the money that he can earn in the film industry. Besides, how long can he go on studying medicine, without completing his studies? There must be a limit to the number of years a student can spend in any medical college."

"So you agree that it would be a good idea for him to become a film star."

"No, No, I don't mean that, Chachaji; by no means. I am just wondering what alternative there is for him; that is, if he does not complete his medical studies."

"No, don't say that, Murli, my son, please don't. He *must* complete his medical studies. Can you not understand that I have spent hundreds of thousands of ringgit of my hard earned money on his studies, what with the capitation fee of US $50,000.00 to get him a place in the first instance? And years and years of tuition fee, living expenses, and money spent on travel both for Ranjit and for his late mother each time she went to visit him in India, not to mention the "donations" and "gifts" I have had to send to his bloody professors just before examinations. They take the money and do not keep their part of the bargain. You know all that."

"That's the kind of trouble that I have had to go through to make sure that *harami* of a son of mine gets a decent education, and what do I get in return? Film star! That's what he wants to become, O my God."

Sujjan Singh was on the verge of tears. He wiped his eyes with the sleeve of his *kurta*. Murli felt embarrassed, not knowing how to react to the rising sense of desperation in Sujjan Singh. Any parent in that situation would have become exasperated. But what was the answer? Sujjan Singh went on to indicate the high expectations he and his family had had in Ranjit Singh, expectations which, in Murli's mind, were totally unjustified, since Ranjit had never been a good student even in school. It was just Sujjan Singh's idealism, Murli decided, the desire to have a son, his eldest son at that, succeed in life. It appeared as if Ranjit Singh's failure was the very symbol of Sujjan Singh's own failure, the collapse of a mission in life. Ranjit had turned out to be a bad investment. If he did not complete his studies, the money Sujjan Singh spent on him would be a total waste. Sujjan Singh's dreams would be shattered. And obviously there would be repercussions.

"You know, Murli *beta* that I have two other children to think of. Jaswant Kaur, well she's not really a problem. Perhaps I can find a decent boy from a respectable family--it doesn't even have to be a Sikh family, as long as they are our people, I mean Punjabis-- and get her married off. All I need to do is to raise enough money for the dowry, some jewellery and wedding expenses. Beyond that it would be her husband's responsibility. But what about Charanjit Singh? He will be finishing his studies soon, and I will have to send him off, also to India, for further studies. I believe he too wants to study medicine."

Sujjan Singh stopped for a moment, wiped a tear on his *kurta* sleeve. Murli heard a sniffle, felt that a dam was about to burst. Genuinely feeling sorry for the old man, Murli got up, and patted him lightly on the shoulder. Sujjan Singh, rising suddenly to his feet, hugged Murli tightly to himself; buried his face in Murli's shoulder. By now Sujjan Singh was sobbing loudly, his tears rolling down Murli's neck. Murli, calming the old man down, decided to let him be for a while. Sujjan Singh sank into his chair, placed his hands on Murli's table to support his head, and continued to sob. Murli went out of his office into the shop, to check on his business. He asked Maniam to order another cup of tea and some *uppuma* for Sujjan Singh.

Two young Malay women were haggling over the price of several pieces of Javanese *batik lepas* with Mohini. Intervening, Murli settled the matter, and the customers made their selection of two pieces. While Mohini packed the goods, Murli gave some instructions to his clerk, Jahubar Ali, who sometimes also doubled as an outstation salesman, handling wholesale transactions. Going into his office again, Murli counted some cash and produced three cheques from his table drawer. The money and the cheques were to be banked, and these items he gave to Jahubar Ali, who began preparations to leave for the United Asian Bank on Beach Street. Murli rejoined Sujjan Singh.

Sujjan Singh had his breakfast in silence. Murli sat at his table, watching him. Sujjan Singh's eyes had reddened. His sadness manifested itself on his face. Murli could not help noticing that Sujjan Singh had aged somewhat in the past two years or so. His face had wrinkled and his flowing beard had grown almost totally white, giving him the appearance of a *sadhu*. The problems created for his father by Ranjit Singh had probably aggravated the situation, he thought. But apart from that, Murli surmised, there was also the sudden death of Sujjan Singh's wife, Kartar Kaur, two years before, only a few months following Sujjan Singh's retirement. That had be a real blow to the old man. Since that day he had grown increasingly concerned about Jaswant Kaur.

Sujjan Singh went to the bathroom to wash his hands, and Murli got the table wiped by Maniam.

"I am sorry to bother you with my problems," said Sujjan Singh as soon as he re-entered Murli's office. "But you know I have nowhere else to turn. You are my eldest son."

"I know how you feel, Chachaji. I am really sorry about Ranjit, and I do hope something can be worked out."

Murli could appreciate the reasons for Sujjan Singh's disappointment. As a trained doctor, Ranjit Singh would have been able to live a decent life upon his return home to Malaya; perhaps he could help his father to educate Charanjit, even if he did not spend money on his father, since Sujjan Singh could live fairly comfortably on his pension, and whatever he earned additionally from money-lending. He could not, of course go on being a money-lender all his life. He had often confessed that the strain of chasing his customers had begun to bother him. Above all, Ranjit would be able to fetch a huge dowry when he got married. Ranjit's failure to qualify as a doctor would be a tremendous blow to Sujjan's prestige amongst the members of his family and his *biradari*. Murli felt that perhaps all these thoughts had already passed through Sujjan Singh's mind at some time or other and that the old man's sleepless nights had been caused by the unremitting, flow of such thoughts. He had mentioned on more than one occasion that he had to resort to sleeping tablets every now and then, and he drank a bottle of Guinness stout or Tiger beer every night before retiring to enable him to catch a few hours of sleep. It was clear that this morning he had emerged from just such a sleepless night. Murli realized that he had to be extremely careful in what was a very delicate matter. He had at all costs to avoid hurting the old man.

Almost as if Sujjan Singh had read Murli's mind, he shook his head from side to side.

"What do you think the Sikh community will think of me? My son a failure? I would have nowhere to hide my face. It will be blackened."

Murli was examining all possible angles to somehow continue the discussion imposed upon him. He was totally inexperienced in such matters. He had to be realistic without being harsh or brutal. Ranjit Singh was obviously not made out to be a doctor. Murli knew, from numerous discussions between the late Makhanlalji and Sujjan Singh over the past few years that Ranjit had gone to study medicine against his own wishes, due to pressure put on him by Sujjan Singh.

"You have your successful business", he would tell Seth Makhanlal, and "your children will get a very good start in life. But look at me. What do I have? I am only a government pensioner, and of course, there is some farming land I have acquired in the native village in the Punjab. That's what I have to live on when I finally retire. Yes, I have decided that I will return to India. My native soil is calling me. You see, I have no choice but to educate the boys."

Sujjan Singh had always had this great desire to return to the Punjab, the land of his forefathers, the richest land in all the world. He was born in Malaya, and had gone thirty years ago to the Punjab to get married to his cousin, Kartar Kaur, according to his own father's wishes, and in fulfillment of promise made by his father to Kartar Kaur's mother. He had never set eyes on his bride until after the wedding. That was the way his father had married; that was the tradition inherited for centuries in the Punjab. Only now, he reflected, things were changing, both in the Punjab and in Malaysia, with the younger generation getting more and more progressive. In the case of Malaysia, the new laws which came after independence, made it increasingly difficult to bring in brides or grooms from India. Hence there were less and less marriages between Malaysian and Indian families. Sujjan Singh was thankful that his elder daughter had been married off several years before, before the demise of Seth Makhanlalji, to a senior clerk in a government department. The dowry he had to give did not amount to much, as his son-in-law was not a professional. They already had two children by now, unfortunately both girls, but at least the marriage seemed to be stable. He was not haunted by any problems from that direction. But the two sons--they had to do better. It was with these hopes that he had sent Ranjit to study medicine, and he hoped that his second son, Charanjit Singh, would do likewise. Charanjit was now in upper VI. His second daughter, however, caused some concern to Sujjan Singh. How would he get her married when, in the next year or two, she finished school and the time came for him to look for a bridegroom? His one hope was Seth Makhanlalji; on him he could depend; but now he too was gone.

Murli, still trying to consolidate his arguments, began to wish
that Sujjan Singh would go away. But he knew it was unfair on his
part to abandon the old man at this point in time. Sujjan Singh
himself showed no signs of leaving. Murli knew that Sujjan Singh
would make his daily rounds, visiting a number of his friends in the
little India area around Chulia Street and Market Street, visit some
of his "customers" to collect installments on loans they had taken
from him, and then return home. That was his daily routine. Over
the years he would visit Seth Makhanlal after completing his rounds,
for the final cup of tea before boarding a bus home to Taman Tun
Sardon.

"Maybe you should allow Ranjit to do what he wishes to, for
a time, Chachaji." Murli ventured a cautious opinion. "Then if he
succeeds, well and good, and if he doesn't he will probably be that
much wiser."

"And if he doesn't I'll be that much poorer, and that much the
subject of ridicule."

"Some of the actors in India have done quite well, uncle." Shashi
Kapoor, Amitabh Bacchan ..."

There was no reaction from Sujjan Singh.

"Several have become politicians, even Members of Parliament,
and Chief Ministers. Look at MGR, Rama Rao and so on. Many
have become millionaires."

"Yes, I know. But have you had a good look at their character?
The way some of them live? Utterly disgraceful."

"There are always some bad hats in every profession, Chachaji."

"Besides, do you think that Ranjit Singh has the makings of
another Shashi Kapoor or Amitabh Bacchan? To start with he
doesn't even have the *shakal*. Increasingly he has proven too that
he does not have the *akal* as well. Perhaps he can play the part of a
clown, though I imagine even that needs some talent. Dreams alone

don't create superstars, beta. Besides all that, who wants to hire a Sikh as a film star unless he shaves off his beard and his *kes*!"

There was a lengthy pause.

"Yes," continued Sujjan Singh, "Yes, Perhaps they can hire him to play a watchman, bouncer or a taxi driver in a film, for a few rupees. Even then, I'm sure they can hire any number of real watchmen or taxi drivers do the job. There's no shortage of Sikhs in those kinds of jobs in India; they don't need someone from Malaysia."

Sujjan Singh was right on every count, Murli realised. Ranjit Singh was not physically striking. He was dark; in fact without his turban and beard he could be easily mistaken for a Tamil. He was shorter, smaller built than the average Punjabi. Ranjit did not have the looks, and no Sikh had really made it big as a actor in the Indian film industry, although there were many Punjabi Hindus and Muslims, Bengalis, U-P wallahs, and Pathans among big names: K.L. Saigal, Dilip Kumar, Hemant Kumar, a whole bunch of Kapoors and a galaxy of well known actresses. At this point, however, he had no wish to contribute anything further to Sujjan Singh's misery.

Murli was trapped. There was little he could do under the circumstances but humour the old man. He knew that if he made a mistake, there would be serious implications for their relationship. The lifelong friendship between his father, and now himself and Sujjan was precariously on the verge of being threatened. He wrecked his brains to look for possible solutions to Sujjan Singh's dilemma. For now, anyway, his brain seemed to have come to a dead

Fortunately, after a few moments of silence, Sujjan Singh himself rose, as if to Murli's rescue. It was obvious that the old man himself could not go on in the present vein.

"Well, Murli *beta*, I think I had better be going now. I have taken too much of your time. You have been very kind, as usual. May God reward you for your kindness."

"Chachaji. I really wish I had some better ideas. But let me think a little. Perhaps in a day or two. . ."

During the following few days, Sujjan Singh did not make his usual visits to Murli's shop. Murli began to worry that something might be the matter with him. On the third day following the meeting in his shop, Murli sent Jahubar Ali to various shops in Little India, places that Sujjan Singh frequented, to find out if the old man had visited any of his friends or customers. It appeared that nobody had seen Sujjan Singh. Concerned at the lack of information, Murli decided to visit Sujjan Singh's house in Taman Tun Sardon the following Sunday.

He learnt from Charanjit and Jaswant that their father had been admitted into the General Hospital. He had developed severe chest pains and his blood pressure had shot up. An ambulance had been called to take him to the hospital. It seemed that Sujjan Singh's condition had stabilized, but he needed to stay in hospital for a few more days, for observation.

It was time for Charanjit Singh and Jaswant Kaur, to take the old man his lunch. They all went together in Murli's Honda Civic. In one of the second class wards Sujjan Singh lay in bed, turban-less, his almost sparse hair tied in a topknot, his beard wild, as he lay gazing into the emptiness of the ceiling as if in a daze. Murli's gentle touch brought Sujjan Singh back to reality. He was glad to see Murli, and sitting up with some effort, made the *anjali* gesture before hugging him; Sujjan Singh could not withhold his tears.

"Why didn't you get some information to me, Chachaji, that you were taken ill? I would have come immediately."

"I didn't want to trouble you, *beta*. It happened in the middle of the night. Besides, there is nothing seriously wrong with me. I am all right. I'll probably be discharged in a day or two."

"At any rate, please make sure you have both my home and business telephone numbers with you, in case you need them for an emergency." Murli handed his visiting cards to both Charanjit and Jaswant. "Please don't hesitate to call if you need help, at any time, day or night."

Sujjan Singh was touched, he patted Murli's hand.

Thank you, *beta*. Thank you for coming to see me." Sujjan Singh's eyes welled up again and he wiped a tear. He had his lunch—a couple of plain *chapattis, dhal,* some mango *achar* and a little yoghurt. When he had finished eating, Murli asked Sujjan Singh if he needed anything. He did not know whether Sujjan Singh needed money for the hospital treatment, but to ask that directly would have been equally embarrassing both to him and to Sujjan Singh. He decided it would be best for him to check with Charanjit before Sujjan Singh left the hospital.

"Nothing, nothing", replied Sujjan Singh. "You know I get free medical treatment. One of the few advantages of having served the government for so many years."

He was quiet for a while.

"Well, uncle, you know if you need anything, you only have to ask."

"I understand, I understand."

The following day when Murli visited Sujjan Singh, he took with him some grapes and oranges. Sujjan Singh was sentimental. He talked about the beauty of his native land, about his youth, about Kartar Kaur and a little about his children. When he began to discuss Ranjit, Murli dissuaded him.

"Don't strain yourself, Chachaji" he said." You need all the rest you can get. Do not let anything worry you now."

There was an extended silence. Sujjan Singh was reflecting upon something or other.

"You know, *beta*. I have only one worry left in this world. My daughter, Jaswant Kaur. The boys will manage somehow, by hook or crook, even if they have to beg or steal, but, should anything happen to me. . ."

Murli was silent.

"You know that I have very few relatives in this country, and I don't get along very well with them."

"Chachaji, nothing will happen to you. Don't worry. I'm sure Jaswant will get a place in a local university, and when she completes her studies there'll be jobs waiting for her."

"It's not a job for her that I was thinking about, *beta*, but her marriage. What do women need to work for? If a suitable match can be found . . ."

"Don't let all that worry you now, Chachaji."

Murli felt uncomfortable. The arranging of marriages was something in which he had no experience at all. Both the marriage of his elder sister and his own marriage had been arranged by his parents.

"I'm sure everything will work out in time."

Sujjan Singh released Murli's arm with a sigh.

The following afternoon he received a call from Charanjit. Sujjan Singh had been discharged and would be resting at home. A week later, at his usual hour of five in the evening, Sujjan Singh entered Murli's shop. He seemed much healthier and less depressed. But he was not cheerful, and significantly, did not greet Murli in English. There was no "Good evening;" just a "*Namaste*". Murli ordered some *teh tarik* for him, and a plain *tosai*. *Uppama*, he decided, would do

Sujjan Singh more harm than good. Sujjan Singh did not raise the subject of Ranjit Singh; neither did he talk about his other children. Instead, it was Murli's turn to offer a suggestion.

"You know, Chachaji, after the last discussion we had in this room, I made some inquiries, about possibilities . . . for Ranjit, that is".

Sujjan Singh did not say anything; he merely listened. It was impossible to say whether or not he was interested in the subject. Murli, however, went on.

"If he does not wish to pursue a long and difficult career in medical studies, homeopathy might be considered as an alternative. It takes less time, and I understand it is easier to handle than medicine, since no surgery is involved; one still comes back as a doctor. I have a friend here in Penang, one of our own people, who is qualified homeopathic doctor trained in India. He's doing quite well. If you wish, we can together go to consult him. But I'm sure Ranjit too can get the information. . ."

"Thank you very much," he said. Thank you for your concern. But, *beta*, while I was lying on that hospital bed, and then resting at home during the past ten or eleven days, I had a great deal of time to think. I have some ideas now. Perhaps I can even arrive at some decisions."

Ranjit experienced a mixture of emotions. Sujjan Singh's quiet calmness seemed ominous. There was seriousness in the old man's face, tiredness, perhaps even resignation. But he seemed to be totally in control of the situation. There was no anger, no violence. The tea came, and he began to drink. Murli joined him.

"I think I have spent enough money on that *haramzadah* Ranjit Singh; he's my son. I cannot deny that; that was something fated; my *karma*. But from now on I will have nothing to do with him. He can do what he wishes. He can be a film star, a member of the Indian

Parliament or even the Prime Minister of India if he wishes. He can become an astronaut, and go to live on the moon for all I care."

Murli was totally surprised at the Sujjan Singh's severe tone. Here was an aspect of the old man he had never seen before. He could sense a mixture of bitterness and steely anger.

"Charanjit Singh will complete his sixth form a few months from now. Following that, I will place some money in a fixed deposit account for him to continue his studies. There will be sufficient for him to complete his medical degree, if he does not repeat any year, that is. There will also be some money for additional expenses. He will not get anything more from me. If he does not wish to study any further, he can do whatever he likes with the money and with his life; he can even join his brother on the moon, if he so wishes. I will not interfere, and I will not expect anything from him."

Murli guessed that Jaswant Kaur's future would next be worked out, and sure enough, Sujjan Singh unveiled his plans for her too.

"I will take Jaswant Kaur to India with me, and there get her married off to one of her many cousins. There have been some letters in the past from various uncles and aunts of hers, showing some interest in such an arrangement. I am sure something can be arranged, in the next year or so. I have saved enough money for any dowry that I may have to pay and for her wedding expenses."

Murli had little sympathy for Ranjit. The decision made on Charanjit's future, although providing little leeway for the boy, also seemed to make sense. At a single stroke the responsibility for his future had been shifted to Charanjit's own shoulders, and Sujjan Singh had washed his hands. But he felt sorry for Jaswant Kaur. She was a sensitive and intelligent girl, and although not an outstanding beauty, she was not bad looking at all. He had no doubt that, given the opportunity to study, she would go far, and perhaps eventually marry well, marry someone of her own choice in this country, not in the Punjab. He would have voiced an opinion, perhaps even a mild and oblique objection, but at this point, Murli felt that Sujjan Singh would not warrant any interference in his plans. Perhaps when he was less upset and in a better frame of mind, Murli thought, he could discuss Jaswant Kaur with her father.

"That will solve all my problems, at least as far as my children are concerned", Sujjan Singh continued. "I myself plan over the next year or two to wind up my business here, collect all the money due to me, and return to the Punjab. I will visit Nankana Sahib in Pakistan, the Golden Temple in Amritsar as well as other sacred places on pilgrimage, and then await my end. At least I will be in my native land should anything happen to me, and my soul will be at peace. Beyond that there is nothing that I or anyone else can do. I leave my fate in the hands of the Almighty Lord of the Universe. The soil of the Punjab has been calling me for some time now, and I can no longer resist its call. I hear the songs of its five rivers. I believe my pension and the income I will derive from the little farming land I own will be enough to keep me in sufficient comfort. And when my days are numbered, Jaswant Kaur and her children can inherit whatever little I leave behind. You see, *beta*, I am very tired. I need peace of mind. I need rest."

Sujjan Singh said the last three sentences in English, slowly, deliberately. Having traced the whole plan out, he remained silent. Murli himself had nothing to say, since the whole decision had come very suddenly, although, he realized, following considerable thought on the part of the old man. Sujjan Singh seemed calm, and even managed a smile.

"Well, *beta* Murli, I think I will leave now. I have to get my collections done, and then go home for some rest. I will see you again."

Murli was amazed at the obvious transformation in Sujjan Singh. Perhaps it was the result of his sudden illness, perhaps his age was beginning to catch up on him, and possibly it was a spiritual transition of sorts brought about by the crisis of his sudden illness, the unexpected arrival of wisdom. Sujjan's Singh's face appeared more radiant than usual, his grey hair almost totally white. In his newly washed and ironed white pyjama and *kurta* Sujjan Singh appeared more than ever before like a saint.

Whatever it was that had so suddenly brought the transformation in Sujjan Singh's personality, as the old man now began to make preparations to leave, Murli could not but admire him for having so quickly arrived at the solution to not just one, but to all of his problems, problems which less than a month ago seemed insurmountable.

Yet one thing bothered Murli—the fate that lay is store for Jaswant Kaur. He was restless on that matter, and even people around him, especially his wife, began to notice it. But no one wished to disturb him in what was obviously some sort of a personal crisis. Most of those who knew Murli, including his own staff, thought it was perhaps some problem with the business, overdue bills and so on. On that score they were totally wrong, for Murli was a steady and honest businessman, a good paymaster in the vein of his late father, Seth Makhanlalji. Yet no one knew how to approach him to find out what his concern was.

On the fifth day following Sujjan Singh's visit to his shop, Murli called Charanjit to make inquiries regarding his father's health. He was concerned since Sujjan Singh had not showed up in his shop. Murli hoped Sujjan Singh was not deliberately avoiding him for whatever reason. That would be a terrible thing to happen. He learnt that Sujjan Singh had, in fact, not left his house in Taman Sardon. He had been mostly resting, and reading passages from the holy book, the *Guru Granth Sahib.* Relieved, Murli nevertheless asked Charanjit Singh to pass a message to his father: that, if he felt well enough and could find the time, Murli would like Sujjan Singh to visit Makhanlal and Sons, at his convenience. No, there was nothing urgent.

The next evening at 5:00 p.m. Sujjan Singh entered Murli's shop, and was greeted by Murli and his staff. Murli held him by the hand and took him to his office, promptly switching off the air-conditioner. He ordered some *uppama* and tea for Sujjan Singh.

"Beta, I was told you wished to see me. Is there anything in particular?"

Murli tried to remain as calm and casual as possible. "Chachaji" he said, "Frankly, I was worried about you, very concerned, following your last visit. I just wanted to make sure you were alright. I am glad that you are in good health."

"Thank you beta, that's very kind of you. Each time I see you I am reminded of your late father. He was a great man. May Bhagwan keep you forever happy, my son."

The tea and uppama came and Sujjan Singh helped himself. Murli noticed that he was still serious, as if some sudden transformation had taken place in his inner being. But he sensed that there was nothing to really worry about.

"Chachaji, I have been reflecting on what you mentioned the other day--concerning your plans for the future." Sujjan Singh remained silent. "Would you mind if I said something?"

"No go ahead. I am prepared to listen. But please bear in mind my situation and all that I have been through. My plan came after deep and prolonged thinking."

"I realize that, Chachaji. I agree with most of what you said. One has to come to some sort of a final decision, especially in circumstances such as yours. As they say time waits for nobody.

Please don't misunderstand me. I am not in any way questioning your decisions. Who am I to doubt your wisdom? But I have one concern. . ."

"Concern? And what might that be, beta?" Murli remained silent for a while, and so did Sujjan Singh. It was Sujjan who spoke first.

"Go ahead what did you have in mind? Rest assured I will not mind what you say. I have always said you are my son. Don't hesitate. Go ahead."

"Chachaji. Its about Jaswant."

"Jaswant? Our Jaswant?"

"Yes Chachaji. You know she is an intelligent girl, brighter than all her brothers. Chachaji, please forgive me if I what I am about to say upsets you. I beg your pardon in advance. I think she deserves a better deal than what you have in mind for her.

"B. . . ut . . ."

"Chachaji I am well aware of your situation and your concerns. I am sure you know that already. But please allow me to go on for a moment. Jaswant will complete her Form V this year. She should go on to form VI and then to a university. I think she will do well."

"But, as you know there are serious implications. My whole plan, how will it work out? What am I supposed to do with myself, with her?"

"Chachaji, you can carry on with the rest of your scheme. I think what you have in mind makes good sense. All I ask you is to leave Jaswant with me and my wife. She is like a sister to me. I have spoken to Malti; she and I will take care of Jaswant, ensure she completes her education and then . . . when the time comes, we will find a suitable match for her, if she has not found someone herself, that is."

Sujjan Singh was stunned at the offer. He did not know how to react. For a moment he felt as if his fond old hopes of getting Jaswant married to Bansilal, Murli's brother, had once again come alive, all of a sudden, miraculously.

"Chachaji, that will spare Jaswant the misery of life in a village in the Punjab as a farmer's wife. It will relieve you of many worries on her account. It will also mean that you will return to Malaysia once in a while, between your travels and pilgrimages, to see her and, naturally, to see us too. Chachaji, I humbly hope you will accept this offer. Think of it as coming not from me but from my late father. I am certain he would have done the same thing had he still been with us."

Overwhelmed, Sujjan Singh got up and embraced Murli, in tears, for a good five minutes, while Murli patted his back to comfort him, reassure him.

"After all that you have gone through, Chachaji, I hope this brings you some peace of mind."

They spent the next hour reminiscing events that passed through their lives during the past thirty years or so, especially those connected with Seth Makhanlalji. The *azan* for the *Maghrib* prayer could be heard from the nearby Kapitan Keling mosque when Sujjan Singh left Makhanlal and Sons, Textiles and General Merchants on Chulia Street. He would be driven home by one of Murli's staff members. Murli could sense a change in him. Sujjan Singh already seemed much steadier than when he had entered the premises at 5:00 p.m.

DEWI RATNASARI

Dewi Ratnasari was pensive as she stood at her window, absorbed in the pouring rain. Her long strands of straight black hair, falling over her young shoulders reached way down her back in sharp contrast to the pale whiteness of her neck and shoulders. She was unusually fair for an Indonesian, thanks to the mixture of European, Japanese and Javanese blood that flowed through her veins. Ratnasari was justly proud of her hair, described by Tanjung, her husband, during the days of courtship at Gajah Mada University as the most glorious head of hair in the East. Indeed, her hair was her most striking feature; it drew the attention of men and women alike, and it left the strongest impression upon those who met her. Only after her hair had registered upon them did they notice her large and attractive eyes, her exciting, almost sensuous physical features. Her colour and the shapes of her nose and eyes led many of her acquaintances to believe that she had origins in Iran or Pakistan. Not surprisingly, her women friends often compared her to the best-known of Bombay film stars, and even to Benazir Bhutto. Only, they said that she, Ratnasari, surpassed in beauty the Pakistani Prime Minister, for her facial features were softer, less angular. Dewi Ratnasari brushed off all these compliments with an air of nonchalance. Inwardly, however, she was glad that Nature had been so generous to her.

The season of rains stretched that year far longer than its wont. It had not stopped raining since early August, and now it was already the 17th day of December. Predictions were that the rains would last at least several more weeks. And then, the hot and dry season would set in. She had little affection for the tropical heat; she recoiled from the approach of the dry season, which brought to her mind images of brown grass, dry leaves and windblown dust. For her, these were symbols of sterility, impotence.

But weather patterns, like much else about the world, were no longer predictable, increasingly so, she noticed, over the past five or six years. But sometimes, in this unpredictability, there were unexpected rewards. This morning, she was thankful for the changing patterns that had brought her such a glorious downpour; for such a downpour of rain from the heavens she would be prepared to exchange almost anything. She was even prepared to accept, along with it, the accompanying bouts of thunder and lightning which sent shudders through her, gave rise in her to an eerie sense of fear.

The rain came in whispering sheets of misty white; strong gusts of wind seemed to mould the flimsy sheets into waves, lifting them lightly on invisible arms. They resembled the curtains in her living room, curtains now equally restless in the wind, their impatience matching the restlessness within her own being, her own being which had become an impatient curtain of gauze through which, unimpeded, the winds and the drops of water seemed to pass.

This image of herself struck her, for she often thought of herself as a nameless part of Nature, Nature that was so gentle and yet so harsh; above all, totally mysterious. It was an abstract and yet a physical presence, a miniscule fragment of the cosmos; and she was a miniscule part of that miniscule part. She could see herself composed of millions of molecules today spread thinner than usual, turning her into gauze each molecule alive and virtually a world in its own right. Through the gauze, the winds of the universe seemed to pass, carrying in their wake indescribable thrills. Today, she had turned into the mountains and valleys of the earth, she had become the whispering trees, the passing clouds with ever-changing forms, she had become the birds that sang their melancholy songs of impending separation; but above all she was the rain . . . In this, her encounter with the rain, lover and beloved had become one in absolute fusion.

The nights and even the days were colder than usual. While it was normal for December to be a relatively cooler month in Penang, this year, the days of December had been almost cold. And the floods too had occurred with greater than usual intensity, inundating the low lying areas in the rural districts and even in the city. She remembered that in her hometown in Central Java, floods were welcomed with open arms by the young and old.

The youthful maidens would descend in rows from their houses into the floodwaters, clinging to their colourful *batik sarung* that turned momentarily into parachutes, splashing the water upon each other, exchanging playful greetings. The floods provided welcome opportunities for the young to meet. Many a romance blossomed during such occasions.

In Penang, there were no water festivals, and even its floods seemed lifeless. They brought in their wake nothing but yawning stench and mud. There were no real rivers in Penang. Yes, she remembered the floods of her youth with fondness. There was romance in them; there was poetry in them, as in the vast singing seas.

As Dewi Ratnasari relaxed, reading once again a collection of her favourite Indonesian poems, the soft strains of Javanese court gamelan filled the hall with the thrilling, almost hypnotising voices of the *pesinden*. She seemed to drift into a state of dreaminess, into the realm of reality beyond. She felt herself drawn towards the plants and trees in the large garden, and towards the pregnant clouds in the overcast sky. The neighbouring hills had become invisible behind thick blankets of mist. Rising from her couch, she drew the long near-transparent beige-coloured curtains. There she stood, by the French windows, for an incalculable length of time, mesmerised, her gaze fixed on nothingness. The dampness of the rain reached out to every fibre in her body, merging with the red stream of warm consciousness within. The living rains and the raging tides of blood in her body sang to the same infinite tune. They had become part of a single harmony. Time and space did not exist anymore. She had transcended both.

Dewi Ratnasari particularly enjoyed the prospect of the raindrops falling on the sturdy leaves of the pair of frangipani trees standing majestic in the western corner of her garden. The leaves became shiny and slippery, with the mingling of rain and the sky's colours. The yellow-white flowers, crisp and radiant, were vibrant, energised. She could feel in them a sensation of joyous exuberance; imagine their perfume filling the environs of the house, enveloping her very being, seeping into every cell in her body.

Each time it rained, she was drawn towards the frangipani trees, their hair bedecked with flowers; she shared with them a common destiny though she knew not what it was. She was aware in vague terms of the mysterious connections existing between the frangipani, death and eternity. The renewed realisation of this link heightened her sense of longing for the unknown, the sense of sadness which constituted the very essence of her personality.

That evening, once again after many, many months, the intensity of melancholy threatened to overwhelm her. She let the dam break; she wept bitterly.

Ever since childhood, Dewi Ratnasari had a special affection for the rain. She had often gone into the sweeping rain with hardly a stitch on her body, had let herself be completely soaked in total surrender. There seemed to her nothing more joyous in the world, even if the adventure resulted in a severe scolding from her parents, or a bout of cold to be carefully nursed away by several days in bed.

As she grew older, she surrendered herself to the rain less and less often, perhaps out of a sense of shyness, perhaps out of a fear that someone would notice her supposedly strange behaviour. She even felt that many ancient gods and goddesses of Central Java were watching her, but of them she had less fear than she had of humans. She was confident that the gods and goddesses would understand the secret urges within her, condone her behaviour, for did not the rains after all bring her closer to them?

About three years ago, a few days before her marriage to Tanjung, the urge had come on so severely that she had no choice but to give herself to the rain, as if in a grand surrender that would bring about a final parting from a lover. She remembered going into the garden, removing her clothes, loosening her luxuriant hair, and making an offering of herself, body and soul, to the dark and violent rain of night. It was rite of some sort, a rite she could not explain even to herself; it was almost magical, an act of worship, whose meaning and intensity remained mysterious even to her. All she knew was that it was necessary. An immense release came through that encounter. She felt spiritually and emotionally cleansed. Instinctively, she knew that every tiny drop she felt as keenly a sense of joyous abandon as did, without exception, every living cell in her being. The rain flowed over every inch of her being, running in little streams in the crevices of her fair and goose-pimpled body. It was the final consummation of her love, for she was certain that once she got married, her relationship with the rain would have to change, perhaps even come altogether to an abrupt end. The very thought of such a breach in a relationship that lasted so long and that meant so much to her brought in its wake unbearable sadness. That night in her room, she had longed for death.

In her childhood, they had told her that she would die one day as a result of her mad devotion to the rain. She was fascinated by that possibility, immensely. With passing time, it became an obsession. It symbolised in her mind the supreme sacrifice — the act of dying for the rain, the rain she visualised as a lover who had total liberty with every square millimetre of her body.

In her dreams, she had many a time seen herself tossed upon the endless waters of the ocean in pouring rain, the waves tall as mountains kissing the very skies; she saw herself torn to pieces, simultaneously with the streak of lightning across the skies and the clash of thunder. That, to her, was the supreme form of heroism, the ultimate sacrifice. In it, there was inestimable joy. She could still recall clearly the innumerable shades of blue and green water and the white crests of the waves. She could still hear the thunderous love-call of the ocean, sweet as the melodious voice of a million simultaneous conch shells. The urge to thus give herself to the majestic ocean and the unstinting rain had never really left her; the suppressed desires drove her to the aching verge of insanity.

Dewi Ratnasari had told no one of her obsession, not even Tanjung. There were times when he came perilously close to knowing of it, but she had been able to keep a secret. He had not been able to hear the call of the blue-green ocean within her, nor see its overwhelming passion. But one night, as she exulted in a dream, Tanjung awakened her. She told him that she had had a dream; she was drowning. Not understanding that she experienced neither terror nor even fear but ecstasy, he nevertheless comforted her. Her secret had remained safe with her. On several occasions when her encounter with the waters in her dreams thus surfaced, she had given similar explanations. Tanjung remained none the wiser.

One morning, out of obviously genuine concern, he had suggested that she should perhaps consider seeing a psychologist. She had laughed at the idea, brushed it off as mere frivolity. She had even pretended to be upset at such a suggestion. Did she, she asked him, have any doubts about her sanity? He light-heartedly brushed the whole idea off. In the core of her very being, however, she knew that he was apprehensive. She had to be more careful, lest she reveal too much. The gentle rain and the boundless, impatient ocean belonged entirely to her. Her dreams and fantasies were her own. She had no wish to share them with anyone.

As Ratnasari stood by her window that morning relishing every rainy moment, her mood of reverie intensified. Once again, after all those years, her suppressed emotions resurfaced — a mixture at once of intense joy, sadness, pain. Once again, she experienced with ferocious intensity the urge to give herself totally to the rain. Her breath came heavily, her bosom rising and falling like that of a maiden anticipating an encounter with a dear beloved. The more she thought of the idea, the more attractive it became. Tanjung had gone to Kuala Lumpur on official business on behalf of the Consulate. Lucy, her Filipino maid, was away for the weekend, to stay with her friends. Dewi Ratnasari was all alone at home. The circumstances seemed perfect for an encounter long overdue.

The idea of going into the rain began to take unremitting control of her. Ratnasari, mesmerised, let her clothes fall one by one. They gathered in a gentle heap on the floor. She was completely naked. She loosened her jet black hair, the best in the East; it reached down to the arch of her lower back, appearing even blacker than usual, in strong contrast to the gentle fairness of her skin.

When she opened the French window, the wind rushed in, lifting her hair, tossing it wildly in every direction, partly covering her face. She did not try to control its abandon. Entranced, Dewi Ratnasari walked out into the garden, proud and naked as a goddess. She stretched her arms upward in homage to the rain, now pouring luxuriously over her body. Excited, she began to circle in dance round and round, encircling the twin frangipani trees by turn at an increasing pace, the dance of ecstasy; the rain, sent down by the heavens just for her, caressed her body. Soon she was on her knees, kneeling, wiping herself with both hands as if to ensure the rain did not miss even a square millimetre of her skin.

The water seemed to penetrate every pore of her glistening body, reaching into the core of her being. Beneath the frangipani, she rolled over and over on the grass, allowing herself to be totally soaked. Strong fragrance of frangipani flowers filled the air; the trees were full of them, their whiteness dotted the green freshness of the grass. Taking now one and next another to her nose she smelled the flowers, intoxicated; overwhelmed by the greenness of grass, by the white fragrance of frangipani, by the music of the singing rain. In the distant, she heard an occasional burst of thunder. It was nothing short of miraculous, the totality of this encounter with the rain, after all those years. And then, she lay still on her back. The tiny rivulets of rain water found their way down the crevices. She could feel vibrant on her skin their cold and gentle tickling flow.

It was a long time before Dewi Ratnasari became totally conscious of her whereabouts. The downpour lessened into a mere drizzle. The wind sent a shiver through her, and she heard the gentle rustle of frangipani leaves. The aroma of freshness was unmistakable, exhilarating after the downpour. Rising, she applied her hands to her face and body as if to gain confirmation of her existence. In the much-diminished rain, she washed off the dirt and leaves clinging to her, tied her hair into a rough bun, placing in it a single frangipani flower. The endless sky was now coloured with streaks of grey, orange and red as the sun descended behind the blue hills. She sighed deeply in what seemed to her a final parting. After a few moments, she went indoors.

The warmth of an extended bath restored her energy, brought back a feeling of life. Now wrapped in her clothes, as she sat on the carpeted floor, she felt a thousand contrary emotions. There was in her a total and exquisite sense of balance, harmony. Outside, the rain had increased again; it seemed destined to last forever. She heard the clap of thunder, the lightning followed soon in its wake in a glorious silver streak across the sky.

Now, more than ever before, Dewi Ratnasari knew, as she had always known, that one day she would go all the way. She would, on a rainy day such as the present, go to the ocean, and altogether naked, she would give herself in supreme sacrifice to the rain and the mighty waves. She would become one with Ratu Lara Kidul, Queen of the Southern Seas.

MEDITATIONS ON A CHARPOY

The early hours of dawn became freezing cold. It had been raining all night in varying degrees of intensity and even now there was a slight drizzle. The dark, biting wind sent shivers through Karam Din as he slept on his *durrie*-covered *charpoy*, doubled up into a cocoon, totally wrapped up in his grey blanket, outside the imposing premises of the Chartered Bank on Beach Street. Karam Din worked as a night watchman.

In the darkness, he could hear the passage of the hours, marked by the turning wheels of an occasional car that hissed through the puddles of water on the road, or the roar of a particularly high-powered motor-cycle. The latter type of sound irritated him; not only did it disturb his sleep, but, on occasions like the present, when he was not really asleep, it disturbed the flow of his thoughts.

"Don't these people ever sleep?" He almost said these words aloud, as if to someone with him.

Soon, the sounds of the night began to change to those of incipient day. There were more people along that stretch of Beach Street, something confirmed by the unmistakable tingling of bicycle- or trishaw-bells. Karam Din could hear loud conversations in Tamil, and an occasional one in Hokkien. He guessed that jetty workers were on their way to work; that early factory workers and travellers who had to catch the ferry to Butterworth and the morning mail-train or buses to points beyond were on their way. The sound of vehicular traffic had begun to get more and more persistent.

The *azan* from the Kapitan Keling Mosque, so highly amplified that it was almost irritating in the dark, confirmed that another day was about to begin.

Karam Din swore under his breath at the prospect of having to get out of bed. It seemed almost criminal that one had to leave the warmth of one's bed. It was such a pleasant time to sleep; there was, in fact nothing even remotely comparable to predawn sleep. It was the veritable quintessence of bliss, thought Karam Din as he hugged his spare pillow closer to his chest, threw his right leg over it.

But Karam Din was restless that morning, and indeed he had not slept well; he had been dreaming of his village in Pakistan, a village he had left forty years ago at the age of twenty-three. He had often had such dreams, in them meeting several members of his family, his deceased parents Elam Din and Tajo. And Fatma, the young bride he had left behind with their newborn baby girl. It had been *kismet* that he should travel beyond the Black Waters, Kala Pani, separate from his family for a short duration to seek a fortune in Malaya, the unknown land beyond the seas, and then to return home. But Fate, in keeping with its reputation, had been inscrutable. Time had passed, in the process taking with it both his parents.

Fatma began to appear in his dreams more and more often; she and their first child, named Savera, born but four months before his departure for Malaya. Fatma had been distraught; feared the worst. In time, their second child, a son, had come into the world during Karam Din's absence, only to leave it immediately even without a name. Fatma had suffered; she had become emotionally and psychologically shaken. And Karam Din's separation with Fatma and their children, with his siblings and all that his native land represented had, over the years, become permanent; even the news that occasionally used to reach him from across the seas had ceased coming.

Such dreams had been recurring to him during the past few nights; in them Elam Din and Tajo appeared as he remembered them forty years ago; and Fatma too, in all her youthful beauty. Karam Din himself had changed over the past four decades, now looking very much as his father did at their separation. But in recent weeks, the dreams had been more disturbing than ever. Again and again, Fatma's persistent appearances had become coloured with violent restlessness. He decided that he should consult the venerable white-bearded Madarasi astrologer, palmist and fortune-teller all rolled into one, who, looking like a saint or an ageing god out of Hindu mythology, sat unfailingly at the corner of Pitt Street and Chulia Street near the small complex of stalls selling flowers and ritual paraphernalia—objects to be used by worshippers going to the nearby Goddess of Mercy temple on Pitt Street or the Hindu Sri Mahamariamman Temple Hindu temple facing Dawood Restaurant on Queen Street.

Each day, Karam Din had seen him there, at that corner, not a whit changed over the years, as if he had attained powers over the processes of ageing and decay, over life and death, attaining immortality, with his motley collection—birds in their cages, beads, playing-cards and other things. Yet each day, Karam Din had hesitated, sensing, perhaps, that something fearsome had been written in the stars, fearing that the crisscross of lines on his palms would reveal secrets he had no wish to know. Then too, he figured that as a Muslim, albeit not as good a Muslim as he ought to be, he should not believe in astrology or consult fortune tellers. It was a practice considered *haram* in Islam. As on many previous occasions, he controlled his urge to visit the sage, decided that he would leave things in Allah's Hands, have *tawakkal*, at the same time making a mental note, for the thousandth time that he should attend to his obligatory *namaz* more regularly. For who knows when Azrael will come knocking on the door?

He imagined the Angel of Death, dark-mantled, accosting him one sunset-reddened evening as he rolled his old Raleigh bicycle to his front gate, asking him to prepare for immediate departure for the dark world of the grave. In his mind, he rehearsed the barrage of questions that Munkar and Nakir would throw at him, with all the drama that was brought into the encounter by the Moulvi Sahib in his village in the Punjab. He sometimes wondered if, except for the colour and perhaps size, Azrael did not, in fact, resemble the *moulvi* himself, so great was the fear that he and his young companions had of the teacher; and then he quickly repented, taking both his hands to his ears and holding his lobes for an instant.

"*Tobah, tobah.* Ya Allah. I beg your pardon."

He must not do that again. But the thought did come into his mind, time and again, for the teacher had been nicknamed Azrael, and even now, as he remembered those incidents, the image of the old moulvi flashed across his mind, all dressed in white, his lips reddened with betel juice.

"May Allah have mercy on his soul," Karam Din muttered.

It was sheer coincidence that had brought Karam Din to Malaya. The tale of how he came to settle in Penang was not really an extraordinary one for those turbulent times, in the late forties and early fifties, the time after the Second World War, the time following the partition of Hindustan into India and Pakistan, and the deaths of millions, including many of his own relatives and theirs in turn on both sides of the new Indo-Pakistan border, in unimaginable ways. He could still remember vividly its very beginnings.

The summer night was warm in Chuharkana Mandi, a village of a dozen shops, a government clinic, a post-office, a police-post and a disarrayed variety of houses, most of them constructed out of mud. The men had gathered in the square near his home, sitting on string *charpoy,* smoking *hookah* and listening to the exciting news and wonderful stories told by a distant relative. This was Mangal Din, thus named because he was born on a Tuesday in some remote year unknown to anyone, including Mangal Chacha or his parents. His parents used to say that two years before his birth almost to the day, for a month or more, continuous rains had darkened the skies and huge floods had drowned the plains of the Punjab. All its five gigantic rivers had gone seemingly insane. There had been massive destruction of life and property. Houses had been flattened; dead animals littered the land. The villagers were certain that it was some sort of warning or even punishment from Almighty Allah for crimes that remained undefined, but were, nevertheless, quite terrible. Pious ones compared the flood to the one experienced by Nabi Nuh, for it seemed almost as great and to last almost as long. There was no doubt that the people had sinned. They must repent. Once things returned to normal, public prayers were held at all mosques to seek Allah's mercy, for the renewal of faith and, more importantly, for the return of prosperity.

Thus, Mangal Din's age came to be reckoned from the flood; and that was about the closest that anyone came to calculating how old he was.

"A year or two more or less, what does it matter?" he used to ask. "Nothing will happen. The world will go on even if Mangoo is not around."

Officially, he was Mangal Din. Those close to him knew him familiarly as Mangoo, while to the younger set he was Mangoo Chacha, Uncle Mangoo. Karam Din called him *chacha* as a matter of habit for that was the customary manner of address for male elders. Karam Din believed that Mangoo Chacha was a distant cousin of his father's. He had never managed to figure out the precise relationship in this particular case nor in many others, for there seemed to be an endless stream of uncles and aunties. To go with every *chacha* there was a *chachi*, with every *taya* there was a *tayi*, with every *mama* or *mamoo* there was a *mamee* or *mausi*, and so on. Some of them, of course, were in no way related to his parents, but the terms of relationship were used anyway as a matter of custom; they were applied even to total strangers.

Mangoo Chacha had gone to British Malaya with an uncle of his and that uncle whom Karam Din knew only as Baba— grandfather or granduncle—returned after two years due to poor health. Baba had in fact, passed away peacefully in his sleep one night in that very village. Mangal Din had remained in Malaya for a while, taking the opportunity, a year later, of coming back for a brief stay to pay respects to his mother, visit his married sisters, pay condolences to his recently-widowed aunt and her family as well as make a round of visits to his numerous uncles and aunts. For all of them, he brought back gifts—clothes, pieces of jewellery, some trinkets. To his mother, upon arrival, he handed a handsome sum in cash. His duties done, Mangoo had gone back to Malaya to stay for another five years. This had been going on for as long as Karam Din could remember. The present return to the village was his first real "holiday" one might say. He planned to remain in Pakistan for six months, possibly longer. Nothing was certain as yet, even to Mangoo Chacha himself.

The most interesting thing about Mangoo Chacha were the endless stories which issued from some mysterious fount within him, stories which seemed to vary and become increasingly exciting with each telling over the nights; stories of how he had become rich overnight in Malaya, that fabulous land of gold and honey. As the *hookah* circulated among the older members of his father's company of a dozen or so village men, gurgling with each elongated puff, Mangal Din related his adventures. To Karam Din, there appeared to be little difference between Mangoo Chacha and Sinbad the Sailor, the intrepid traveller and adventurer *par excellence*, whose adventures had excited Karam Din since the earliest of his schooldays. Karam Din had no doubt that in old age, when he had retired from seafaring, Sinbad the Sailor looked exactly like the grey-bearded, white-turbaned Mangoo Chacha.

The visit to Calcutta, the unimaginably huge city, seemed to have left a particularly strong impression on Mangoo Chacha. He related how he reached Calcutta after what seemed like an endless train journey from Lahore; but it was the description of Calcutta that was the real highlight.

"You should see the size of the buildings", he said. "Many of them touching the very skies. But the strangest thing about the city are its people–*lakh* upon and *lakh* of them. Somehow, they are different from us; the men are short and dark, and the women, they are pretty enough, but nothing compared to our Punjabi damsels. No women anywhere come close to ours, both in beauty and in build, I can tell you", he added, "and by Allah who watches and hears everything, I don't tell the untruth. I have seen the world with my own pair of eyes. But to come back to the Bengalis, and more precisely to their language, my God, I couldn't understand a word of it, so strange it seemed. Luckily, there was always someone who could speak Urdu or Punjabi, and *haan*, here and there even a few of our own people, mostly Sikhs and an occasional Musalman. I must tell you, in spite of whatever happened in 1947, I was always glad to meet one of our own, a Punjabi—Hindu, Sikh or Musalman—in Calcutta. There were many more Hindus and Sikhs than Musalmans. It was in fact a Sikh *jawan* who saved my very life. Otherwise, I would have died of starvation, not knowing where to find decent *chapatti* and *paratha* during my first day or two in that city. Imagine having to eat rice and smelly fish all the time, like the *sala* Bengali *log* do. I would surely have grown thin as shrivelled sugarcane waiting for my ship those sixteen days. But the city; it's incredible."

He mentioned some strange sounding names, Howrah Bridge, China Bazaar and so on, which at that point did not make any sense to Karam Din. But just listening to the glories of Calcutta, his imagination went wild. He had been to Lahore several times, and that was the only real big city in the world, as far as he was concerned, though he was aware of the existence of others – Delhi, Karachi, Bombay, and even London, where the *Angrez log* came from, mostly from the books he had to read in school. He had studied for three years in all, and could read and write a little Urdu. As far as the *Angrezi* language was concerned, he knew just a few words and phrases, and those too he had picked up here and there, mostly from the radio, for he had never studied English in his village. It was only the big cities that had *Angrezi* schools.

Karam Din loved Lahore immensely. To him, there was no city like it on earth. He knew well the *mohalla* around the railway station with its narrow streets, where his cousins and other relatives lived. He had seen some of the Mughal architecture — the tombs, the beautiful gardens, the great Badshahi Masjid, the tombs of Aurangzeb and Anarkali, the incredible noisy bazaars, ancient and modern, the latter with their broad roads crowded with motor vehicles, *tongas*, and even camel-carts as well as some of the gleaming white buildings constructed during the British raj. Could any place be more wonderful than Lahore?

But this was the first time he had met anyone who had actually been to Calcutta, and he longed to be there one day. According to Mangoo Chacha, beyond Calcutta there were Chittagong and Rangoon, and finally Penang, in Malaya. Karam Din had never before heard of these places; but he knew that many of his friends' relations had been to Singapore. Geographically, of course, these places meant nothing to Mangoo Chacha's audience. They were merely fanciful names representing unknown places lying somewhere in the far reaches of the imagination. Only now, with the details filled in to some extent, did they become real places in any sense of the word. Their very existence was confirmed by someone no less than Mangal Din, their very own Sinbad.

Karam Din had never been in a ship before, and that in itself was a source of wonder both to him and his listeners. Mangoo Chacha's descriptions were amazing in detail and rich in metaphor. How a huge metal bowl carrying hundreds of passengers had travelled over vast distances of blue, green and black waters for seven days and seven nights without sinking with all the weight it carried in is belly. There was really nothing that Mangal Din could compare a ship like that to. The closest image that came to him was that of Nabi Yunus in the belly of a whale derived from the *moulvi*'s sermon, and that's how he described his own seemingly precarious situation on the Penang-bound ship. There were so many of these floating on the oceans, crowding the ports he had visited. It was just incredible.

To his listeners, none of whom had ever travelled by sea, and a few among them who had never even boarded a train for the village did not have a train station, Mangoo was not only a weaver of wonderful tales, he himself became a fairy tale figure; someone straight out of the *Hazar Afsane* or *Shahnama*. They could not imagine how water could extend for such vast expanses that it took seven days and seven nights to cross, water that kept changing its colour. Penang, they concluded, must be at the end of the world. This notion was promptly corrected by Mangal Din.

"No, brothers", he said, "Ships go on, beyond Penang to other places, Singapur, Chin, Bertania, Amrika, and only Heaven knows where else, sailing over the endless waters. I tell you Allah is great. Its only when you go across the ocean in a ship that you realise God's immensity.

"But isn't it dangerous?" someone asked.

Mangal Din, to sustain interest in his stories, promptly added, "Of course, there are dangers. Why should I deceive you? First of all, there are the whales. I remember seeing a whole bunch of them together for the first time in my life about halfway to Penang, each as huge as a hill. But that is nothing. There was no danger to the ship or to anyone on board, for they did not come near us. The sea itself was the source of real anxiety. In the waves that rose as high as mountains and sank as deep as valleys, the ship seemed to touch the very bottom of the ocean and then rise to kiss the sky. I tell you, it was frightening, so frightening that I have no words to describe my fear. Compared to the immensity of the ocean and the open sky, the ship seemed no bigger than a *kuali*, such as the one *dhal* is cooked in. People got sick and started vomiting. At night, when asleep, on the deck, they rolled on the floor, back and forth like corpses thrown out of their graves. But can you believe it, even on the ship there were *hakim*s and compounders—people like our Zafar Mian here, and a real dispensary? The sick recovered once the sea became calm, and the medication took effect. And those who died, for there certainly were some who died, those who died were wrapped in shrouds and thrown into the sea after prayers had been said over them."

At this his audience expressed shock, and Mangoo Chacha's response was prompt.

"Well, what did you expect the ship's crew to do? You didn't expect that the dead would be kept on board together with the living, did you? The bodies would begin to rot and stink in no time."

"Were they Musalmans or kafirs?" someone asked.

"Both. Both Musalmans and non-believers, of course, and the funeral prayers were different accordingly."

Seeing some doubt, and hearing the muttering among members of his audience, he added. "Yes, yes, brothers, sea-burial is allowed, even for Muslims. I am certain it is stated somewhere in the *Quran Sharif.* In the case of Muslims, the *namaz* was led by a properly qualified *moulvi*. You see, the ship carried moulvis, Hindu *pandits* and even a Christian priest or two."

Mangoo Chacha, seeing the rapt interest in his audience, and he himself the focus of attention, made all manner of demands; this is where Karam Din had a role. After all, at twenty-three, he was the youngest member of the company. Each time there was such a gathering in the open *maidan* near his house, he was told to be around—to replenish the *hookah*, to get the *paan* prepared or to serve snacks. Mangoo Chacha's sessions were special, and Karam Din made sure he did not miss any. He usually found a place on one of the *charpoys* but faced discreetly away from the elders, or he sat on the floor, leaning against one of the carved legs of a *charpoy,* listening keenly. He could not really participate in the discussions; they were meant for the elders. Occasionally, he did ask a question or two, receiving an appropriate response from Mangoo Chacha or a retort from one of the elders.

"How about some *phirnee?* I really haven't had decent *phirneee* in a long while." Mangoo Chacha asked, and later on, "How about some more *masalah* tea. Wah! The tea prepared by Karam Din's mother Tajo Bhabhi is really out of this world."

"Help yourself to another cup." interjected Elam Din, Karam Din's father. "We'll get some more when the teapot is empty."

And so the *masala* tea, prepared by Tajo and Karam Din's newly married wife, Fatma Bibi, kept on flowing; the sweets, *pakora* and *samosa* had to be purchased from Qasim's little *mithai* stall round the corner. Qasim was the village's best known *halwai*. For Elam Din, the additional expenses did not really matter. How often does one get to entertain a celebrity like Mangal Din, someone who had crossed Kala Pani, and returned, not once but several times, with these unending tales, and also fabulous wealth?

Mangoo Chacha mentioned that in that fairy-land of British Malaya, everyone was rich, most of them in the towns lived in *pakka* houses, and even the village houses were made of good wood, for money grew on trees.

"Really?" asked someone. "How incredible! You mean real currency notes?"

"Don't be stupid", said Mangoo Chacha. "I'm talking figuratively."

To illustrate his statement, he took off his new pair of yellow Japanese slippers, purchased in Malaya, and bent them double. He had brought in two dozen pairs in several colours and was hoping to make a small fortune from them, as well as from a great many other items, some worthless ones, by selling them to friends and relatives in the village and in the neighbouring town. He knew the fascination these village-*wallah*s and town dandies had for foreign goods. He came well-prepared to at least recover the cost of his ticket back to Penang. The other items, such as jewellery and so on, had also made him some savings for they were much cheaper in Malaya than in Pakistan, and more important, they were foreign.

"Rubber," he said, pointing to the Japanese slipper, still held high in front of his face. "That material, from which this *chapal* is made, from which a thousand other things are made, comes from tall trees that produce sticky white milk. Now have you heard of that before? Trees producing milk, like our village cows?"

Ignoring one or two observations of incredulity, he went on.

"The trees, planted in rows, stand like thousands of *sipahi* on parade. All people have to do is to make a slice in the bark of a tree with a sharp knife every morning, and the milk begins to flow. All the workers do is to collect the white rubber juice, send it to a factory for processing into sheets. There's a lot of money in it, I tell you. Many in Malaya have become *crore-patis* just from rubber. Even the roads are paved with rubber, and on them the traffic flows, sarr, sarr, smooth as silk."

To answer persistent inquiries and requests for clarification, he had to go into the technicalities, explaining in his own crude fashion, within the range of his own limited knowledge, how rubber trees had been introduced into Malaya from God knows where by the *Angrez log*, and how that land had become wealthy. He described the rubber trees and plantations, and the process of tapping the white sap, which then coagulated and when processed became Japanese slippers. And not only Japanese slippers, but bigger things too, like motor-car and lorry tyres. It must be mentioned that not all his information was accurate; but that did not matter. No one knew the difference. He made it a point to stress that the plantations were run not by the native Malays, nor by Punjabis, of whom there were few in Malaya, but by the Madarasi Tamils. Again, of course, none of his friends of that night had seen Madarasis, and some description was in order.

His audience was fascinated. They had heard of the jewellery, the transistor radios, the clothes, and everything else that Mangoo Chacha had brought back from that land of plenty, for such stories quickly spread through village gossip-channels. Those things were all within the realm of credibility. But trees producing milk, like cows? Now who ever heard of that? The whole village was agog with conversation of the return of Mangoo Din. And now listening to his story, from the horse's mouth as it were, their conviction was total.

Late into the night, evening after exciting evening, the stories kept pouring out. One night, it was rubber, the next night, tin and on the third night, with a few new faces, it was rubber again. The description of Calcutta and story of the actual journey were repeated countless times, and as the days passed, more and more information on his actual stay in Malaya was considered to be in order. The tea continued to flow, the sweetmeats to be brought in turn by various members of this little group, and the gurgle of the *hookah* could be heard late into the Chuharkana Mandi night.

Mangal Din was a celebrity. He made the rounds of the village, was invited for lunch or dinner by various families, including those of relatives and their acquaintances. Later on, he visited his relatives in villages neighbouring Lahore, Shaikhupura and Layalpur, stories of his travels and of the wealth of Malaya reached far and wide, getting more and more interesting and exaggerated as they went along. For now, the villagers were more interested in these tales than those of *Heer Ranjha* or *Mirza Sahiban*. Those age-old classics were always there, but how often does one get someone like Mangoo Chacha, with his brand-new tales, spilling as it were from his *pagri*?

"The *sala Angrez log*! Why did they not plant rubber in the Punjab when they were here? They did nothing for India. All they did was to create a thousand religious problems between the Hindus and Muslims; they robbed the land, sent everything to their *sali* queen in London, so that Bertania could become rich and powerful. All they left behind were a great many half-caste *harami* bastards."

His audience could not but agree with him, seeing the reality around them. In the Punjab, there were no rubber trees from which money could be collected almost effortlessly each morning.

The preparations for the wedding of Mangal Din's elder daughter proceeded smoothly. She was to be married to some distant cousin from a different district. The *mangni* had taken place while Mangoo

Chacha was still in Malaya. That kept him busy in Chuharkana Mandi for a while. He had to ensure that everything went smoothly and the wedding would be a memorable one, within his own *biradari* at least. He would only be returning to Malaya after the wedding.

It was about two months after his arrival in Chuharkana Mandi, that Mangal Din first mentioned the possibility to Elam Din of Karam Din being sent along with him to Malaya. By then, the story sessions had begun to stale, though the gatherings still took place as usual. That, after all, was the way of life in the villages of the Punjab. Anyway, what does one do after dinner? What better entertainment than to gather, talk about this or that, chew betel-leaves, drink cup after cup of *masala chai*, smoke the *hookah*? In such gatherings, there was real fellowship, and from them many a thing developed, including marriages.

The subject of Mangal Din's own marriage had been broached one night during such a gathering. And the marriage of his only daughter was similarly planned. No, not planned, but discussed and then announced. Mangoo Chacha had the bridegroom in mind many, many years ago. It was the son of his own elder sister, from a village near the city of Layalpur. She had mentioned the possibility of the marriage soon after Mangoo Chacha's daughter was born. Mangoo Chacha had no problem agreeing to the match. It was only a matter of confirming it by exchanging some *mithai* and a few rupees in coins. This was done when his daughter was three years old.

"Think of it, Elam *Bhai*," Mangoo Chacha had said, after broaching the subject. "There's plenty of money to be made in that distant land across Kala Pani, believe me. I can get Karam Din started in some small business, the same way I myself did."

Mangoo Chacha had been a small-time textiles dealer, peddling his wares from place to place on a bicycle with a group of others, mostly Sikhs, and was by now apparently doing quite well, having set up a permanent stall in the Piccadilly Bazaar in Penang. Well enough to return to Pakistan with all the goodies and to spend time doing no work; just living on his seemingly countless Malayan dollars. His stories had considerably impressed Elam Din. Mangoo Chacha's life in Malaya was certainly more exciting than the life of a simple farmer that he lived in the village of Chuharkana Mandi.

"I am doing this only because of our close relationship. Why should I bother if I did not have an especial affection for you, and for him, whom I regard almost as my own son? In fact, if my own son Jumma was of the right age, I would take him along with me too, to Malaya". He puffed on the *hookah*, as if to stress his point, and to allow Elam Din to reflect on his proposal.

"Yes, think about it, *Bhai*. Take your time," he said, in between extended puffs. "I will not be leaving for a while yet. I don't think you will ever regret listening to my advice. Have I ever suggested to you anything that wasn't sound?"

As they days passed, Elam Din mulled over the idea of sending his son away to the foreign land across the Black Waters. Karam Din was his eldest son; then there was Fazal Din, the younger son, and he had three daughters, only one of whom was married. When he mentioned the idea to Tajo, she immediately reacted unfavourably, almost becoming hysterical. She did not like the idea of parting from her son. Furthermore, if Karam Din were to go away what about their daughter-in-law, Fatma, who was expecting her first baby? There were so many questions that had to be answered, so many things to think about before any decision could be made.

Neither Karam Din himself nor Fatma were consulted on the matter, however. His father had once asked him for an opinion. But it was not really a serious attempt to seek a solution to the dilemma, for on one side was the continuing life of near-poverty that the family had been living; on the other side lay untold potential. Karam Din, though relishing the idea of travel, of seeing the great city of Calcutta, and lands beyond it, was unable to make up his mind. The matter was too complicated for him.

Karam Din took a peep from under his blanket at the grey sky. It was still dark, but he knew that the dawn was just bursting to be born. It had been delayed somewhat by the rain. This, he could tell from the Bus Sekolah that had started moving about, the trishaws that had increased in number. Yes, it was getting to be morning on Beach Street, but Karam Din could still spend some time in bed, enjoying the warm relief that his blanket provided from the morning winds. There was no hurry. He still had about an hour and a half before getting up from bed, and packing his things, leaving his *charpoy* in the store room at the back of the building. On Sundays and rainy days, all these formalities took a little longer. Usually, he was all ready to leave by about 7.30.

For many a day, Elam Din had been restless; his unkempt beard had grown thicker than usual, and greyer; his being suspended between the current oppressive reality and the dreams that though normally cost nothing, these days seemed to be demanding a heavy price. At night, when everybody was in bed, Karam Din would hear his father pacing the floor of the open yard onto which their rooms opened. Tajo, if she happened to get up, would boil a glass of fresh cow's milk or prepare a cup of tea for him, and he would spend the summer nights thus walking or seated on the edge of his *charpoy* dreaming, thinking of the future. His own life was almost at an end; Karam Din could take care of himself. Fazal Din would soon be out of school and would somehow be able to manage along, being a man. But what about Tajo? What about the two girls? Something had to be done soon about the marriage of Rahimah; she was already seventeen. And Karimah was not far behind. She had already passed her fourteenth birthday. There were many questions, important ones, in the father's mind during those restless nights.

These questions were discussed during subsequent meetings between Mangoo Chacha and Elam Din.

"*Bhai* Elam Din, What was the hurry of getting Karam Din married?" Mangoo Chacha asked. "After all he's only a boy. He could have waited several more years. It is the girls we have to worry about."

He saw Fatma Bibi as the principal hindrance to his otherwise almost faultless scheme.

"I had an obligation to her father. You know that. Your sister Tajo and I had given our word to her father when Fatma was just a child. We could not go back on that word of ours. It would have been unthinkable. Besides, as you know, her father died early; her mother had nobody else to turn to; no grown-up sons to take care of her. So we had to help. We had to have the marriage take place. Please don't question that decision, my brother. I gave it a great deal of thought at the time the marriage was confirmed. And what's the use now of talking of things that cannot be changed?"

The gurgle of the *hookah* seemed to put a final confirmation to these grave statements of Elam Din. Mangal Din realised that he could not deny the truth of what Elam Din had just told him. At the same time, he was sure that his advice to the old man was sound, and also that a way could be found out of what seemed like an impasse. He decided to let things lie for some time. This would also help in allowing Elam Din to reflect further on the situation. Besides, he too had things to do—countless visits to make, extend personal invitations in the traditional manner to all his relatives in so many different villages—and so on. The day for the wedding was fast approaching.

One fine summer night, about a month later, the decision came, almost miraculously. It was Mangal Din again who had the bright idea.

"Elam *Bhai*," he said, "I have seen you worried, and I understand the reasons for your concern. But don't you think that if Karam Din went to Malaya for a year or so, no, perhaps for two years, at the most for three, it would be of considerable help to you? The three years will pass before you know it. Imagine, whatever money he sends you can be used to marry off the second girl. That means that you can begin planning from now. Look for a suitable boy, start the negotiations, while Karam Din sends you enough money for the dowry and the marriage expenses. That would lift a tremendous burden from off your head."

"But . . ."

"But, you were going to say "What about your daughter-in-law, Fatma Bibi? Is that the problem?"

Elam Din was silent. Mangal Din knew; and he continued.

"I have the perfect solution for that problem too. You see, I have been thinking more creatively. Your daughter-in-law can stay here for the duration of the two or three years, and Karam Din, when he returns after his stint, can take her back with him, should be decide to go to Malaya again, as I am sure he will. She will have her baby soon, and the baby will keep her, as well as you and Tajo Bhabhi's company. I am sure your hands will be full. There will be no time to get bored or to worry. If Karam Din is away for a while, that should not make a big difference. Time will fly, and before you know, your son will be back here in Chuharkana Mandi again. After all, it is for the welfare of the whole family. I sincerely think you should give this thought serious consideration now. The more you delay, the more complicated things are likely to become."

Following this discussion, for the first time Elam Din seriously
sought his son's opinion on the matter. Late one summer night,
Elam Din, Tajo and Karam Din sat on a couple of *charpoy* on the
flat roof of their house. Fatma did not join in the discussions; she sat
on the floor at a distance, her head covered with a *dupatta*, discreet,
listening, intent on not missing a single word.

"I think your Mangoo Chacha has a point. How much can we
earn from this oil-press business? Already, I am of little help, and
soon I will not be able to do even the very basic things. If the stay in
the *pardesi* land is to be short, then, I think we can all bear up. I am
sure you can make some worthwhile amount of money in no time,
if what your Mangoo Chacha has achieved is any example. After all,
you are young, and if your Mangoo Chacha is there to guide you,
things should be easy enough."

Karam Din had little to add to this. His thoughts went in
many different directions. Overall, he began to sense the feeling of
excitement building up in him. The accounts of his travels and of
Malaya given by Mangoo Chacha had been infectious. And the fact
that Mangoo Chacha himself was making good money, there was
enough evidence that his stories were no fairy tales.

When it was finally agreed that Karam Din should go to Malaya
for a while, Fatma's heart sank. She was on the brink of tears.
Covering her face with her *dupatta*, she went down into her own
room and cried, cried uncontrollably. Although she had had a feeling
for some weeks now that the decision would be made for Karam
Din to leave for Malaya, when it actually came, the shock was
unbearable. She had no idea of what distances lay between her village
and that unknown land that now was taking her husband away from
her. In between their village and that strange foreign land lay the
wide expanse of Black Waters, Kala Paani. She had fears too, that
the separation would be longer than planned, that perhaps Karam

Din would not return, that he would forget her, perhaps even find another, more beautiful woman. A thousand unpleasant thoughts troubled her soul, and as she mulled over and over them each of her fears seemed to multiply its inherent terrors a thousand-fold.

Tajo came in to console Fatma, and later, Elam Din visited her in her tiny room, a room that he had never entered before in his daughter-in-law's presence. He tried to comfort her, patting her back several times, taking her head into hands and kissing her forehead through her *dupatta* while she sobbed.

Karam Din himself did not know how to react to the manner in which she reacted to the news of his imminent departure. He was tongue-tied, awkward. Later, when they came together, despite her pregnancy of three months, that night's love making was the best in a long while, as far as Karam Din was concerned.

As the days passed, she became resigned to the idea of separating from her husband. She grew much quieter, and altogether more serious, as if in just a few weeks she had matured, even grown old, an old spirit in a young body.

Fatma Bibi, like several other young women that he was allowed to mix with during the days of his youth, was a distant cousin. She was the daughter of one of his mother's cousins, who had been married to a cattle farmer in Hazara district. This cousin of his mother's had, upon the rather early demise of her husband, moved into Chuharkana Mandi to stay with Karam Din's family. Fatma Bibi was, in fact, brought up together with him. By the time this move took place, there was already some talk about his marrying her when the time came. He understood that his own father had given his late uncle, Fatma's father, his word; and nothing in the world could shake that. To Karam Din, it did not matter one way or another, whether he married Fatma or some other from amongst the several cousins touted as potential candidates. Although he liked one or two other girls and had even flirted with them occasionally, nothing more serious by way of a romance had developed from those encounters. In his eyes, Fatma was pretty enough and her manners were refined for a village girl. His precise familial relationship with her was too complicated for him to work out, and he rarely bothered about it. To the whole village, she was merely so-and-so's only child.

His marriage to her had taken place on a modest scale, for the family could not afford a grand marriage. He was twenty-one and she was seventeen. That was a year and a half before Mangoo Chacha returned to CM.

Karam Din tried to remember the kind of relationship he had had with his wife. It took a while for her to respond to him. He figured that perhaps she needed time to adjust, for they had lived in the same house almost as if they were brother and sister. After the initial period of shyness had been overcome and their love making became regular, he found her physically exciting. They settled comfortably into their new situation as husband and wife, and she had no real adjustment problem as far as the family was concerned, for she had lived in the same house for some years now. Even between her and her in-laws, there was a close relationship. She did not have to observe the *pardah* when her father-in-law was present. It was different, of course, with the other elders and young men of the village. In their presence, she had to maintain a discreetly low profile, hide her face behind a *dupatta*. When she did go out, which was seldom, she had to cover herself in her black *burqa*.

Thinking back on those times with his wife, Karam Din felt both a tinge of excitement in his loins and sadness in his heart. He gave deep sigh, held his pillow closer to himself in the cold of the Penang morning. Imagining the young Fatma was in bed with him. He could almost recall the smell of her lithe body, feel the long strands of her hair covering his face. In his imagination, his hands explored her nineteen year old body.

Following the serious discussions between Elam Din and Mangal Din, it was decided that Karam Din should wait until the birth of his first child before leaving for Penang. Mangoo Chacha could not delay his departure. Immediately upon the completion of his own daughter's *nikah*, and once she was firmly settled in her new home, he left. A few days before he took the train to Calcutta, on his last visit to Karam Din and his father, he gave whatever advice he considered suitable regarding Karam Din's oncoming journey to Penang. The advice mainly concerned the travel documents, which he had to obtain from Lahore, money required for travel, train and sea tickets and so on. Mangoo Chacha gave a strong assurance to Elam Din that when he received confirmation regarding Karam Din's travel plans, he would make all necessary arrangements for his accommodation, and so on in Penang.

The birth of Karam Din's child brought in its wake disappointment. His mother Tajo in particular, was visibly upset that her first grandchild was a girl. She had all along prayed Allah for a grandson. This feeling of disappointment somehow also spread to Fatma Bibi, who went into a serious bout of depression. Karam Din decided that perhaps now that the child was already in this world, and his departure imminent, Fatma was over-reacting, playing it up. She became increasingly reserved. She would talk to people only when necessary. In these moments of acute stress, Karam Din did not know how to react. He did not have any experience in such matters, and so could not help but fumble. It was his father who served as a pillar of strength in the family, the source of great comfort for both Karam Din and Fatma Bibi. As if to counter the feelings among the other members of the household, he even boasted to his neighbours that in Allah's eyes, a granddaughter was superior to grandsons for with the birth of every female child in a family, Allah opened one of the doors to Heaven. The grandsons, he said would come in future.

Four months after the birth of his daughter, Karam Din left Chuharkana Mandi by train to Lahore and Delhi en route to Malaya. The delay was caused mainly by Karam Din's concern for Fatma, for, although she recovered some of her composure and even a sense of acceptance, she seemed to have lost forever her jovial nature. By the time he boarded the bus for Lahore, however, she was pregnant again. It was decided that in spite of Fatma's second pregnancy, Karam Din's plans be maintained; the sooner he went off the better, before the responsibilities related to the upbringing of his children became acute. And these were not the only potential problems. His parents too were growing old.

A telegram was sent to Mangoo Chacha announcing his plans. Mangoo Chacha himself, in fact, had only written once since he went from Chuharkana Mandi to Penang. Though his silence worried both Karam Din and his father, they concluded that Mangoo Chacha must be well. Perhaps he had nothing important to write about.

Karam Din remembered both the sadness of parting and the excitement of new experiences that lay before him. Fatma Bibi could not be easily consoled. Her father–in–law kept reminding her that the separation from her husband was but temporary; he talked of the unlimited opportunities that would be available for Karam Din in Malaya. He had given the matter careful thought before agreeing to let his son go, he said. It was for the betterment of everyone. If Karam Din worked hard and was prudent enough the whole family could look forward to a better future.

"See how much your Mangoo Chacha has achieved in just a few years. Besides," he said, "Karam Din will be coming back soon, perhaps in a year or two at the most."

During those crucial days, Karam Din's thoughts were heading in another, altogether different direction. Would he ever see his parents again? His father, in particular, seemed to be ageing fast, and his health was not very good. Though there was at the moment nothing serious, one could never guess what the future had in store for him and the rest of the family. His mother was healthy and he felt no concern on that score.

In the weeks immediately before their separation from each other, both the father and Karam Din, though they seemed to have the same thoughts, did not express them even to each other. Karam Din tried to drown his thoughts in the preparations for the departure, and for the rounds of obligatory farewell visits to relatives in different towns and villages. He had to go to Lahore several times to make arrangements for the journey to Penang. The most important of these were to visit the local branch of the immigration office and obtain some sort of pass which would allow him to leave the country and to go to Penang.

As the date for Karam Din's departure grew near, there was still no news from Mangoo Chacha from across Kala Pani, but Elam Din assured his son that everything would be alright. He had total faith in Mangal Din. A couple of younger brothers and cousins, including Jumma, Mangoo Chacha's son, were given the honour of accompanying Karam Din by bus to Lahore, where Karam Din would catch the train for Delhi and then transfer to another for the long journey for Calcutta.

DATUK HANG TUAH

Datuk Hang Tuah bin Alang Thamby Kecik was thirty-eight years old, as yet a bachelor, seeing no good enough reason to get married, and by any account filthy rich. Immaculately dressed, as was his wont, in a beige Seville Row suit and a red tie, he had had a busy final November week in his more–than-posh glassy office on the 57th floor of Wisma Merdeka—the nerve centre of his considerable business empire.

The Annual Meetings of several of the companies he was involved in were due to be held in the first quarter of the coming year. Normally he spent as little time as possible in the office—at the most perhaps two to three hours a day twice a week, calling in some of the managers for the purpose of obtaining progress reports. Often, as a matter of routine, he would just drop in for a few minutes for a cup of coffee or a light-hearted chat with his secretaries. That he felt was more than sufficient. After all, it was not exactly his job to run the companies.

His businesses were being run for him by a host of managers, assistant managers and what not—a few British and American citizens who served as advisors, as well as Malaysians—Chinese, Indians as well as Bumiputeras. The Bumis had been given choice positions according to company and even national policy, as well as to fulfill the requirement of quotas.

Datuk Hang Tuah, of course, saw the necessity for such regulations as a means of assisting members of his own community improve their lot in the Malaysian society, to redress some of the injustice, which, rightly or wrongly, according to the official view at least, were the result of unfair British colonial practices which resulted in the suppression of the Malays to the advantage, in particular, of the Chinese. Thinking of what might have transpired in his community's past, Datuk Hang Tuah would of a sudden wax nationalistic, and, on suitable occasions, would condemn the British as well as the Americans as ruthless colonizers of weak nations. Thus he assumed, that in every case the colonized people, including the Malays, were altogether blameless for letting the *orang putih* in. He had neither the time nor the inclination to ascertain the facts regarding Malaysia's history, and he assumed that all books on the subject were by British hands and therefore not worth reading.

As far as his business was concerned, given the choice, he would have preferred no more than a handful of Bumi workers at any level, particularly in management. Experience had, however shown him that, for the sake of greater productivity, a good mix of workers from various races was a distinct advantage. His offices were actually over-staffed, and in these economically difficult times, in particular, he felt that there was a tremendous waste of resources. Limited and tactful retrenchment was now possible, but he had to avoid retrenching too many Bumi workers, for that would lead into difficulties with the authorities. Besides that he would not be repaying the debt that he owed to the Party and the community.

In his principal office in Wisma Merdeka, the headquarters of his business empire as well as in many of his businesses themselves, the Malays, always the best dressed, were the most visible. That was the way it was supposed to be. But it was really the fewer non-Malays, who maintained a lower profile, who kept the office as well as his businesses going. Without them he would long ago had become broke. Like him, every administrator in the country knew this for a fact, but had to bear with it.

As the year drew inexorably to a close he came in more regularly, spending most week-mornings in his office and sometimes, much to his displeasure, even remaining there after lunch. He would rather take an afternoon nap in the comfort of his Bukit Damansara mansion and spend the early hours of the evening on a tennis court or in a swimming pool at a luxury hotel.

Datuk Hang Tuah relished luxury in every form, and given the wealth that had come his way he could both afford it and, if necessary at all, justify it to himself. Starting off as a mere graduate teacher, he had had seen his fortunes change rapidly. He was a beneficiary of the New Economic Policy that, during the past quarter of a century or so, had turned perhaps thousands of unknown persons like him into multi-millionaires and even billionaires. He estimated that before the current economic crisis he was worth close to a billion ringgit.

Much of the wealth came from several large parcels of land given to him in strategic areas of Kuala Lumpur by a former Menteri Besar, who happened also to be a distant cousin. These parcels of land he had developed with the assistance of various individuals, non-Malays in most instances, with hardly any effort or capital on his part. Many of the office and apartment blocks had been sold off and the money reinvested in various sectors—plantations, construction, industry, and hotels.

Yes, he had been fortunate. There was in him no feeling of it being at all wrong, no sense whatsoever of guilt. It all came from his good fortune—the fact that he was a Bumiputera, that he had been at the right place at the right time, and of course, that he had had all the right connections. His active involvement in politics too was an asset, but once he had accumulated wealth, and the directorships in various companies began to come his way, he gradually withdrew from active politics. There was no longer any necessity for him to be actively involved.

Officially, his stand was that he had no time, that he had to take care of his businesses and so on. He continued to make contributions, mainly financial, to the party and towards specific projects of the party, including the construction of its multi-storied State headquarters complex in Shah Alam. This was a means of showing his gratitude to the party, and also a means of continuing to maintain the goodwill of its leaders.

There had been several such busy weeks, and Datuk Hang Tuah expected the pressure of work to remain until Christmas and the New Year celebrations. At that time, everything would shut down for a week or more. The approaching fasting month of Ramadan would also mean a further drop in output. He really wished he could just go away somewhere for the next two months or so to avoid all this stress. But all he could spare at this time was perhaps a week.

As suggested by Datuk Shahrul Mizad and other friends of his at the Malaysian Embassy in Manila, Datuk Hang Tuah would probably go once again to that city, where the Christmas and New Year season was particularly exciting, the women were ever-enchanting, and the Pilipino language rolled languidly on the tongue—"*kamustaka?*","*maraming maraming selamat po.*" He had a special fondness for the Philippines, where he had spent two years studying for a Diploma in Business studies. He had completed a bachelor's degree, in Malay Studies at the University of Malaya in Kuala Lumpur, and upon graduation had worked as a temporary Bahasa teacher. He had then received a MARA scholarship to Indiana University in the United States. By the end of the scholarship period, and even by the end of the second extension he managed to obtain to his grant, he was still struggling to complete a Masters programme by course work. With the ending of the maximum time allowed by the university, he had no choice but to return from the United States without the Masters degree. The little chance he had of becoming an academician ended at that point. Still, the exposure had been important, and exposure was one of the aims of his scholarship; so he had gained something after all. If nothing else, the stay in Indiana and the visits to various parts of the United States of America had improved his spoken English and opened up his mind.

It was at the suggestion of Datuk Shahrul Mizad, a fellow course-mate of his at the University of Malaya, that he decided to do a Diploma in business studies. The college he selected was a relatively unknown one. The chances were that he would, from that college, get a diploma with minimal effort. This was the assurance given by Datuk Shahrul Mizad, who himself, since his posting to the Philippines had enrolled for a part-time course in management at that very college. After all, thought Hang Tuah, a diploma is a diploma. It did not matter which institution issued it. What was the point of struggling when something could be obtained without effort? It was always best to take the easy, the least stressful way out. As time went on that somehow became his "philosophy." Hang Tuah was, however, infinitely glad that a door had been opened for him into the Philippines, a country of which he knew almost nothing before. He had come to love it; the Philippines had countless attractions for a bachelor like him, and to the Philippines he went each time life became boring in Kuala Lumpur. For the first time in many years the Datuk felt physically run down during the past week or so. This was basically because of the *gawat* situation, which meant that he had to concentrate, he had to devote some energy to his work, both activities which were anathema to him, and totally contradictory to his nature. He never saw the real necessity for work, and in fact, in the true sense of the word he had done little or no work all his life. The sort of concentration that he had to devote to the documents before him these days was abnormal.

But these were unusual times for the country and, with the country, for Datuk Hang Tuah and for every other Malaysian citizen. He could not totally escape the impact of events around him. Fortunately some of his wealth was placed in a Swiss bank account, and some of his landed property was in Australia and New Zealand. With the *gawat* situation those overseas assets had more than doubled in value in ringgit terms. Thus he escaped the fate of most Malaysians, whose fortunes had diminished in the past months.

However, the fact that the Datuk's companies had loans from various banks, some in foreign currencies and the fact he was involved in many companies as Director or as Chairman, and even as guarantor of loans meant that the situation could not be altogether ignored. It was potentially quite serious.

Normally, when things were going well, all he had to do at this time of the year each year in preparation for the upcoming meetings, was to sign the stacks of documents placed before him above his neatly typed name, without even so much as even glancing them over. Given the current economic slow down things were expected to be fiery at the meetings, what with most of the companies in which the Datuk was involved declaring losses. There was pressure to remove some of the Directors of the companies concerned, especially those who were seen as inactive, ineffective, and no longer able to use their connections to bring benefits to the shareholders. In short those who could not deliver the goods.

Datuk Hang Tuah was a Director of so many companies that he himself was never really certain of their number, receiving monthly allowances the total value of which he was equally sure of. He assumed that if he but received five thousand ringgit per company the total would be close to a quarter of a million ringgit a month. *Alhamdulillah.*

Now that trouble was brewing in some of those companies, he had to make at least some preparation to face the shareholders, to give the impression that he was involved, that, like them, he was affected by he downturn, that he could appreciate their frustrations, etc. etc. In short he had to impress the shareholders; he had to make them believe that he was still an asset to the companies concerned.

He could, no matter what steps he took and how much preparation he made, clearly see the number of his Directorships diminishing in the coming months, with the corresponding diminishment of his income. The potential problems were serious, especially in his own companies which were losing money in the millions of ringgit. The spectre of bankruptcy loomed large before him, causing him sleepless nights. In the long term, there seemed no way in which this could be prevented, unless he brought back his overseas reserves. That would be high folly at this time. Any drastic change would, of course, mean a change in his lavish lifestyle, and a loss of face, especially among the Bumiputera elite. Something had to be done, at least to save his Directorships. He did not wish to join the increasingly long list of bankrupt Datuks. There was a joke going around the country that Kajang jail these days had a heavy concentration of Datuks.

The least he could do was study the summary reports, get briefing from the various managers, and when the questions were raised, to answer them intelligently, explain away the losses in such a manner that the shareholders do not feel they have been cheated by the management and Board of Directors. He would almost certainly need the assistance of his "inner cabinet", call them in early next week before proceeding into any business at the office. So, his work for the coming weeks or perhaps months was already cut out for him. For now, however, he could relax, look forward to the weekend. Tomorrow was Saturday and he would have the opportunity of playing a round of golf with Datuk Tengku Alamudin. He took his golf very seriously for it was at golf rounds that opportunities both for advancement in business as well as in other ways often availed themselves. Why, a single game could result in gains of hundreds of thousands, even millions of ringgit—just a whisper into the right ear, like that of the Datuk Tengku, for instance, could open so many doors, just as reverse whisper into his ear from the Datuk Tengku could. He wondered if he should this weekend approach Datuk Tengku Alamudin for a loan just to tide the bad times over. He would think seriously about that possibility, perhaps mention to the Datuk Tengku that he may need some assistance without mentioning a figure, and gauge his reaction. The important thing was for him not to play golf too hard. Although he was a good player, he knew when he had to deliberately lose a game. "Sacrifice a golf game and make a huge gain" became, for him, almost a motto.

This policy had assisted him in the past, financially as well as in other ways. That was how, for instance he had managed to become a Datuk. There was no really worthwhile contribution from him to the country. Nothing. Just to the party. And that as well as his friendship with the right kind of people had resulted in recommendation and the title. With that many new doors had been opened to him, and he had also managed to open doors for others as well as collect a number of important new friends.

Golf had been responsible for many of his directorships of companies, companies whose very existence he was unaware of before, and even now, as Director, he could off hand, recall the names of perhaps a dozen or so companies in which he was involved. The names for his own companies were carefully selected—Syarikat

Sinar Bulan Gemilang Berhad (BGB) for instance and Syarikat Sang Surya Berhad (3SB or Sangsu) as well as Syarikat Matahari Naik Berhad, Syarikat Malam Berbintang Berhad, Marikh Sdn Berhad, and so on. Other companies belonging to him incorporated Hang or Tuah in their names—Hang Setia Sdn Berhad, Hang Bijak Sdn Berhad, Hang Khazanah Sdn Bhd, Tuah Murni Sdn Berhad, Tuah Laju Flying Company Sdn Bhd, Tuah Kukuh Hartanah Sdn Berhad, and so on.

The attraction to the company names incorporating the sun, the moon and the planets had come about following his vehement interest in astrology. This interest developed from the fact that a Chinese fortune-teller had once told him that his good fortune came from the name he shared with the famous Melaka warrior, Hang Tuah. Although he knew that his father had named him after Hang Tuah the Melaka warrior, up to that point he did not give his own name any serious thought. It was not a very common Malay name, but that was about it. He certainly thought it was better than being named Abdul or even Muhammad something.

But he was soon to discover that he shared with his historical namesake not just the name; there were other glaring similarities or parallels between his life and the life of his venerable predecessor. Apparently the date of birth too was common between this modern day Hang Tuah and his ancient namesake. While the mythical Hang Tuah had had three close companions, Datuk Hang Tuah had three half-brothers of whom he was also very fond. There were of course several sisters and half-sisters as well, but they did not come into the reckoning in such matters. Like him his three half-brothers had been able to make a fortune in business, sometimes through his, Hang Tuah's, efforts. Hang Tuah always felt that in today's world the wars were waged not on battle fields but in corporate boardrooms. This came to him from books on Western business houses, tycoons and outstanding personalities.

The correspondences between the two Hang Tuahs, the historical personality and our hero, seemed to go on and on, much to the fascination of Datuk Hang Tuah. He soon became obsessed with the Melaka warrior; he began to see greater similarities between their two lives, lives lived centuries apart. It became one of Datuk Hang Tuah's burning passions to extend the list of such parallels between him and his predecessor to the utmost. To this end he consulted all and sundry, and he read *Sejarah Melayu* and *Hikayat Hang Tuah* again and again almost as if these works documented his own family history.

In his plush office he had a large portrait of Hang Tuah of Melaka, in traditional warrior dress, specially commissioned from a leading local artist with an especial interest in historical personalities, hung on the wall behind his desk. And side by side with this portrait was one of his own, equal in size to the first, painted by the same artist. The two pictures were framed in gilded wood so that they looked exactly alike. The only major difference was that while Hang Tuah of Melaka was dressed in traditional Malay warrior-costume, Datuk Hang Tuah wore a dark grey Seville Row suit.

A particularly imaginative eye could no doubt discern the similarities between the two personalities thus portrayed—the heroic look, the glint in the eyes, the sparse beard. Yes, there were unmistakable resemblances. Interestingly, visitors to his office often pointed out, much to Datuk Hang Tuah's chagrin, another common feature between the two Hang Tuahs—the fact that their features seemed to be to Chinesey rather than those of typical Malays. Were there not stories in circulation that Hang Tuah was in fact Chinese, from the same clan as Hang Li Po?

Datuk Hang Tuah, naturally, did not believe that every one of the similarities and parallels between him and the historical Hang Tuah were mere coincidences. There surely must be something more than mere accidents in all of this. If he had been a Hindu, he would have most certainly and vehemently claimed to be a reincarnation of that ancient hero of Melaka. But being a Muslim, as least nominally, he liked to think of himself as a liberal and modern believer, member of a new breed of international Muslims who did not necessarily agree with some of the traditional views of orthodox Islam, embraced modernity, and more importantly, quickly grabbed without the slightest hesitation the opportunities that came his way.

Of course one could never tell for sure if there was such a thing as reincarnation. Like much else taught by the various religions this concept too could not be proved. But Datuk Hang Tuah certainly liked to believe that there was some mysterious connection between him and his venerable predecessor of the same name. He developed a great fascination for that remarkable figure, and definitely felt a passionate kinship with him. He equally admired Maharaja Lela who disposed off Birch, and certain other more recent or modern-day Malay heroes, all of whom he considered equally reincarnations of the eternal Hang Tuah, with him being the last, and perhaps the greatest—all coming to claim their birthright which had been lost to foreigners, often sold to them for a song, so to speak. Literally, in fact, as history could easily witness, the birthright had often been sold for a woman. The long line of such Circe-like seductresses could be traced from Hang Li Po down to today, coming in different races and nationalities, different guises. Into their laps kingdoms had fallen.

Datuk Hang Tuah admired women, of course, like all rich and famous men and although he had had more or less serious, and occasionally tempestuous, relationships with several local and foreign women, including upcoming film starlets within the country, with whom, as a class, he was particularly fascinated, because they seemed to live at the same time in several levels of illusion and reality.

But with all that involvement, he had managed thus far to remain unmarried. Not that he had given thought to the possibility of marriage. For him, it was vitally important that his immensely significant line, with tremendous potential, be continued. It was also important that it be continued through noble blood. He would have nothing less. Surveying the field for possible or potential brides, then, he had identified three candidates from different royal families, not all three by any means outstanding beauties, and one of them a divorcee. In this instance, his inclination was to go for prestige and wealth rather than beauty, for after all wealth, if properly maintained, would outlast any woman's beauty. And woman's beauty he could obtain by means other than marriage, as he had done throughout most of his adult life.

No formal approach had been made as yet to the families of any of three princesses. They were not even aware of Datuk Hang Tuah's plans to approach them. He needed more time to make up his mind. He saw no need to hurry.

As far as he knew the historical Hang Tuah had never been married—up to this point in his life another parallel with himself, a parallel which the venerable Chinese master had not pointed out. Hang Tuah had taken Tun Tijah from Pahang but she had been handed over to the Sultan of Melaka. Hang Tuah had had no plans to marry her. Similarly when he went to Majapahit to fetch the supremely beautiful Galuh Chandra Kirana, it was to bring about a union between her and his Sultan. Hang Tuah had, of course, finally gone, according to the legend, to live forever with the mysterious Princess of Gunung Ledang. No one knows if he met her and even less if he married her at all.

Surely the time would come for Datuk Hang Tuah too to meet his own modern version of Puteri Gunung Ledang—perhaps one of the three already identified, perhaps someone else. The important thing was that whomever he finally married must be the possessor of true blue blood.

He wondered if the historical Hang Tuah were alive today in modern day Malaysia what he would be like. Was it possible that he would be the very mirror image of our own Datuk Hang Tuah —successful politician and businessman? Datuk Hang Tuah believed that, finding in the possible situation yet another parallel between the Melaka hero and himself. Well, why not? Surely he could not be a keris-wielding warrior in this day of Science, Technology, the Euro, Cyberjaya and the Petronas Twin Towers? After all the Keris and much that the Keris symbolized was consigned these days to museums, of which the numbers were increasing by the day with discoveries in places such as Lenggong and Beruas. Much lesser symbols—more decorations than symbols—they could also be seen in Central Market souvenir shops. For Datuk Hang Tuah, the new culture was the culture of wealth; everything else had to fit into it or around this culture.

These ideas regarding the possible connections between Hang Tuah and Datuk were, in fact, first triggered off by a Chinese fortune teller, the Venerable Master Chin Chye, who had come visiting Malaysia. Datuk Hang Tuah had gone to consult him in Melaka. At the very mention of his name Hang Tuah by the Datuk, Master Chin Chye had mentioned possible historical connections between the Melaka warrior and Datuk Hang Tuah. Datuk Hang Tuah hand the fortune teller suitably rewarded, financially as well as with a title from one of the States. Master Chin Chye was also appointed one of the Datuk's many personal international advisors, ready to come into his office for consultation at the shortest notice. These advisors looked after his health and spiritual welfare. Apart from Master Chin Chye there was a silat expert, the Mahaguru Hamid Don, Swami Sivananda Shastri, who was a yoga exponent, Indian astrologer as well as an expert in ayurvedic medicine, a leading bomoh, Wak Soedarsono, who hailed from Penerogo in East Java, and Abdullah Mansoor al-Falaki a notable star-gazer of Indo-Arab extraction often appointed by the authorities to look out for the moon before the beginning of the fast of Ramadan or Hari Raya Puasa. It was a powerful gathering of highly qualified persons, those who found a place in the Datuk's inner circle. While each member had a special role according to his own qualifications, the Datuk seemed to have a special admiration for Master Chin Chye.

Yes, there was much to admire not only in ancient Chinese fortune-telling and *fung shui*, or in the Chinese way of doing business, but also in other aspects of the Chinese culture and ethos. There were a whole lot of companies with Chinese names such as Triple Happiness Sdn Bhd and Middle Kingdom Sdn Bhd. Other companies were better known by the acronyms such as Falcon, Risecon, ABC (reminded him of air batu campur), BBC (reminded him of the British Broadcasting Corporation) which he once admired vehemently but gave up admiring due to their biased reporting about Malaysia's achievements. Then there was Air Laju Sdn Berhad, Lautan Dalam Sdn and Awan Larat Sdn Berhad, companies with romantic sounding names taken from nature, not to forget Syarikat Manggis Terbang Sdn Bhd to honour Malaysian fruits. He vaguely knew what activities or businesses they were involved in. What did it matter, as long as the profits and allowances for being a Director kept coming in.

As long as he did not allow the current economic downturn to dampen his spirits, life was exciting for him. He was looking forward to the night out to the week-end, with a small group of business associates. Traditionally they would spend part of the evening at one of the city's massage parlours, his own favourite being a really classy one, but one with a strange name—Lucky Fortune Massage Parlour in the Bukit Bintang area—then for a night out at one of the city's leading discos such as Nocturnal Melody, not far away from the massage parlour, eventually retiring, possibly with a pretty companion. When Hang Tuah had such company, he would of course not go to his "official residence", but stay the night in the suite of one of the many hotels belonging to his friends, or at one of their private bungalows. Occasionally they would drive to Port Dickson and stay the week-end at one of the beach bungalows. It was best to keep his self-respect, at least among his servants and the occasional *kampung* relatives who, seemingly coming from nowhere in particular, stayed over at his house. The precautions were necessary for obvious reasons.

It was already 12.15 p.m. and he looked forward to his lunch appointment with Datuk Mohideen Merican, a property developer from Penang, at the Istana Hotel. There were half a dozen joint development projects in which he was involved with Datuk Mohideen Merican, as well as in some instances, with other partners. Apparently some of them were in serious trouble. The two Datuks had been meeting regularly in recent weeks. He pressed the button of the speaker phone.

"Rohana, could you please call Azhar to bring the car?"

"This is Sally, Datuk. Rohana left a little early to go to the clinic."

"What's wrong with her?"

"It's her son who is not well, Datuk."

"I see, Okay, get Azhar."

"Yes, Datuk. Datuk, Just a reminder, Datuk, You have an appointment this afternoon, Datuk."

"Appointment? Really?"

"Yes Datuk. You are meeting Mr. Desmond Teoh from Hong Kong at three. I believe he called a few days ago to confirm the meeting."

"Desmond Teoh? Yes, yes. Of course. Is there any file for me to look at?"

"Yes, Datuk. Shall I bring it in now."

"Yes, but quickly. I have to go soon."

Sally was by far the most attractive of the staff members in Datuk Hang Tuah's office—with long straight hair, an outstanding figure and a good height, fair skin, and a smile that somehow seemed to linger long after she had left, like the perfume from her body. Sally was also efficient, in a way that, he had to admit, only the Chinese can be. He could not, of course, help comparing her to the Malay staff in his office, most of whom did very little more than warm their seats. This was especially the case with Rohana, his personal secretary. Rohana was a senior member of his staff, having worked for him for more than ten years now. She had only recently received a raise which even he knew she bloody well did not deserve. It was a sympathy raise for she had had yet another baby to add to her half a dozen—half a dozen in the last eight of nine years for she had got married only after joining Datuk Hang Tuah's firm. The raise had nothing to do with her work. In fact if her work was taken into account she would probably have long ago been retrenched.

The Datuk resolved that he must do something for Sally, increase her salary a little, even though measures were being taken to trim staff as well as cut expenses. He could afford to spend a hundred or even two hundred ringgit more every month in this instance. And he told himself that this time, it was for no other reason than the fact that Sally was a good worker. Nothing to do with his infatuation with her, of course.

Sally had long the subject of his lecherous attentions. Each time he had flirted with her or approached her for a date, however, she had turned him down, and as the weeks and months passed she had begun to avoid even his glance. He knew that she had a regular boyfriend, a Chinese doctor, perhaps she was already engaged to him, the lucky bastard. Datuk Hang Tuah felt frustrated at the very thought of not being able to possess Sally. It was to him an insult, for he realized that no matter how wealthy or powerful he was there were limits to what money could buy. If only she had been a Malay, things might have worked out differently, he was sure.

Even Datuk Hang Tuah himself could not help realizing that, as far as his attitude, or more precisely range of attitudes, one should say, towards the Chinese were concerned, there was a serious contradiction within him. On the other hand, he hated the Chinese as a race, regarded them as totally unscrupulous, perhaps unconsciously felt threatened by them. Fortunately the NEP had provided for those like him a protection against the Chinese, at least in business, and the system which developed, thanks to the May 1969 incident, had guaranteed them political supremacy as well. But the Chinese could not be suppressed altogether. Yes, he hated the Chinese. On the other he could not help admiring their business skills, their shrewdness, the fact that they worked hard and accumulated wealth so easily on their own initiative, and the soft smooth skins of their prettiest women.

In his own businesses he depended considerably upon the co-operation of the Chinese, although personally he hated to think that he was involved in "Ali-Baba" type deals. He justified such deals to himself by saying that, after all, the Bumiputeras were new in business and that they had to learn from others. In the case of Malaysia, this really means that they had to learn from the Chinese. Moreover both the Chinese and the Malays benefited from such arrangements. So "Ali-Baba" arrangements were temporary in nature, a necessary evil which would eventually, at some unknown date in the distant future, be altogether phased altogether out.

Sally brought the file into his office. Her appearance was like a breath of fresh air after all the stress that had been building up inside him all day long.

"The file, Datuk."

"Thank you, Sally."

He noticed her impatience to get out as soon as possible, and wished he could detain her a little longer, if only to feast his eyes on her.

"How are things with you, Sally?"

"Fine, Datuk. By the way, Datuk, there's a note written by Rohana in the file. You have further documents relating to the meeting with Mr. Desmond Teoh, Datuk."

"Yes, yes. Now that you tell me, I recall that I have some documents. I think I put them in the filing cabinet. Thanks for reminding me. I will look for them after lunch. If I am late please ask Desmond to wait for me."

"Yes. Will that be all, Datuk?"

"Yes Sally. That will be all. Thank you so very much."

The Datuk followed Sally with his gaze, his eyes riveted to her. Her figure really stood out in the *sarung kabana*. What a pity the *sarung kabaya* had gone out of fashion, giving way to all those shapeless *baju kurung*. He blamed it on the changing atmosphere in the country brought about by the *ulamak* types, the religious fanatics. "The hypocrites", he almost muttered aloud, "They should spend more time looking at beautiful women. That could teach them a thing or two about God and His creation."

Datuk Hang Tuah enjoyed watching old Malay movies, and one of the principal attractions in those films were of course the *sarung-kebaya*-clad heroines—Latifah Omar, Maria Menado, Saloma and soon.

Yes, he must remember to give Sally an increase in salary for her efficiency. He would get hold of his Manager in charge of Staff matters as soon as possible. Hang Tuah wrote a note to himself on his memo-pad.

The discussion over lunch which he had with Datuk Mohideen Merican was a disappointment. The Penang project was sinking deeper into trouble. Datuk Mohideen had, in fact, come to seek Datuk Hang Tuah's assistance. The two Datuks, partners in the project with a Chinese developer in Penang, needed further loans from the United Commercial Bank. Datuk Hang Tuah told his visitor that he would look into the matter. No firm promises were made. There was, in fact, very little that Datuk Hang Tuah could do at this time, with bank loans becoming tighter by the day. The amount required was really quite substantial, and only a recommendation from the very top could, if at all, secure it for Datuk Hang Tuah. Even then he would have to break the loan application into several smaller packages and approach several different banks. It was an impossible task.

And with several of his own companies in trouble if he really could get hold of such substantial sums in unsecured loans, perhaps through the assistance of Tengku Alamdin or the Tan Sri himself—and even that possibility seemed remote at this time--he would rather use the money to save his own ongoing interests rather than a project that had barely begun to take off. But whichever way he looked at it, it looked to him like a disaster--the Penang project. The several million ringgit already given as deposits for the land would go down the drain, the deposits paid on the machinery orders from overseas would be lost. He and Datuk Mohideen Merican had now to be prepared to be sued for breach of contract, or whatever else lay in store for them. But he could not, in the meeting with Datuk Mohideen, make any of this too apparent. He merely said that he would do his best. The real situation would have to be unfolded subtly, stage by stage.

With these worries Datuk Hang Tuah was on his way to his office in Merdeka Towers in his brand-new black Mercedes 380. He was developing a throbbing headache. He swallowed some pills with a sip of water. A little further on, all of a sudden he asked Azhar to turn around, and to take him to the lake gardens. His head was pounding. He needed time to still his mind. He wished he had not made the appointment with Desmond Teoh.

Datuk Hang Tuah, left his coat in the car and walked into the gardens alone. After a short walk, he sat down on a bench, and loosened his tie. The cool surroundings still exuded freshness, even though it was already past two thirty in the afternoon. Fortunately the sun was not too bright as the rains had been coming during the past few weeks due to the La Nina effect. The Datuk sat on a bench, took a few deep breaths, closed his eyes, relaxed, and listened full-focus to the water trickling into the pool from several small streams. The sound of the water seemed to wash away some of his worries. For a moment he felt like calling his office on his hand-phone to cancel the appointment with Desmond Teoh; then decided he may as well get it over with. Nothing much was likely to come out of that meeting any way. Twenty minutes later, somewhat refreshed and a little less tense in his head, he knotted his tie, and walked back to the car. He was now ready for Desmond Tan.

"Back to the office, please, Azhar. I have this stupid appointment with a Hong Kong Chinaman."

Azhar had been with him for more than ten years. He was more of a friend than a driver.

Rosnah informed him that Desmond Teoh was already waiting for him in the guest lounge. He had come early. Datuk Hang Tuah needed a little time to freshen himself up and also to locate the file on Desmond Tan's proposal, glance it over as fast as he could. Even if he could not discuss it in detail, something he did not plan to do anyway, he had at least to give Desmond Tan the impression that he had given the matter his serious consideration.

A few minutes later he called Rosnah to send Desmond Teoh into his office. There was a knock and Desmond Tan entered with an attractive young lady.

"Ah Desmond. How nice to see you again. How the time flies. We met when. . . six month ago, in Taipei. Remember the two nights we spent in Peitou?" Datuk Hang Tuah rose to shake hands with Desmond Teoh.

"You have a good memory, Datuk; very important to have a good memory, especially when you do big business." Desmond Teoh laughed his raucous laugh. "Yes, yes we met in Taiwan six months ago almost to the day. You have a good memory."

"And this is ...your Secretary?"

"No, Datuk. This is my niece, Sharon, Sharon Hang Si-To.

"Ah, your niece. How exciting." He shook Sharon's hand, pressing it firmly and taking it to his lips kissed it. "How exciting." Desmond Teoh nodded and laughed.

Sharon was pretty in a general sort of way, with a good figure revealed to advantage by her *cheongsam*. She had long hair and a pleasant smile which revealed fine, even teeth. He could not help comparing Sharon to Sally. There were similarities, but Sally's beauty was of a more subtle kind. In her there was an inner glow that seemed to be missing in Sharon.

He led his visitors to the settee, placing his right hand on Sharon's back, something that Desmond noticed. There was more nodding, more laughter. Things seemed to have started on the right note as far as he was concerned. Datuk Hang Tuah was obviously interested in Sharon. That should help him in his business dealings with the Datuk. "Come, let's sit down, why are we standing?"

Sitting in front of him, Sharon formed a pretty picture. Through the *cheongsam* slits, her thighs were exposed. She tried to keep her legs together, kept tugging at the hems of the *cheongsam*.

"So how are things with you, Desmond? How long are you here for this time?"

"How long I stay depends entirely upon you, Datuk. Sharon would like to spend a few days here in Malaysia. . .Kuala Lumpur, Melaka, maybe even in Penang. We came to Malaysia only to see you, Datuk."

"I see. So Sharon, what do you do? I mean do you help your uncle in his business. Or do something else?"

She merely smiled. It was Desmond Tan who took the opportunity to provide the information.

"Sharon is a movie star, Datuk. Not a major one yet, but she's still young. . ."

"Movie star? Oh my goodness. I should have guessed. She is so very beautiful, and has that something . . . something special about her." Hang Tuah was now really excited. "You know I have met some of our own starlets, but compared to you . . . I can see that they have very little . . ."

Sharon was flattered and embarrassed at the same time. She flashed a smile. Desmond Tan nodded.

"Thank you very much Datuk. You are being so very kind. I keep telling her she has potential."

"She certainly has. I can see that. So, have you been in many films?'

Sharon smiled. Once again it was Desmond who responded.

"Yes, Datuk, in many films, in Hong Kong as well as in Taiwan, but she has not played the heroine yet. I think two or three offers for leading roles will be coming her way soon. Her last role was in *Romance of the Three Kingdoms*, very famous Chinese story. You must have heard, Datuk . . ."

Datuk Hang Tuah was not really listening. He was flirting with Sharon. Who cares for *The Romance of the Three Kingdoms*, when there's romance in the air, right here?

"How interesting, you were saying the romance. . . ?"

"The classic book, Datuk, *Romance of the Three Kingdoms*."

"Yes, yes, the book, the book, the romance, the book and the romance." There was laughter all round, and more nodding. Desmond Teoh felt very good at the way things were going.

Rohana brought in a tray of tea and some biscuits. Hang Tuah poured tea for Desmond, Sharon as well as for himself. Desmond Teoh was getting anxious to broach the subject of the proposed project with the Datuk, but he had to find a way to divert the Datuk's interest from Sharon without appearing to do so.

"Datuk, Sharon will be here for a few days. Maybe you can have dinner with us some time, and also show her around—Kuala Lumpur, Melaka, anywhere in the country, if you like . . . and if you have time. I am sure both of you will enjoy it. It appears you are interested in films.

"Of course, I am interested in films. I am familiar with western, Malay and Hindustani ones."

Sharon was really keen to meet you. That's why I brought her along with me this time, Datuk."

"Really? What has he been telling you about me? Nothing bad, I hope."

"No, No. Nothing unpleasant, only the best things, Datuk."

Desmond Tan laughed again, nodding.

One thing became clear in Datuk Hang Tuah's mind. That Sharon Hang Si-To, this young actress or whatever she was from Hong Kong was being offered to him on a platter. He knew the Chinaman would not give anything in return for nothing. He was certain the time had come for Desmond Teoh to put pressure on him about the contract proposal. It had, after all, been sitting around for quite some months now. Still, the Datuk tried to relish the moment, delay the discussion for a little, if only for a few moments longer. For now he was willing to believe that, of course, Sharon Hang Si-To was an actress. That was the most exciting and logical thing to believe. Call it illusion, call it reality. The world itself was an illusion.

"Where would you like to go, Sharon? Yes, I will certainly be your guide, and your chauffer."

Sharon smiled. The Datuk laughed. Desmond Teoh nodded knowingly. It all seemed to be settled. She was his to possess for the next two or three days, and nights. It would be a great relief from his office routine. Datuk Hang Tuah decided that very night he would take Desmond Teoh and Sharon out for dinner, and then let Desmond return to his hotel. He and Sharon would spend the rest of the evening in New Paradise, the best disco in the city, before adjourning for the night, to a hotel suite. He could already relish the pleasures awaiting him. He was sure that would be one of the most memorable nights of his thirty eight-years. In the morning he would drive Sharon to Port Dickson and Melaka, returning to Kuala Lumpur on Sunday. They drank the tea.

He was now ready to deal with Desmond Teoh's business proposal. But he knew that nothing could be settled this time, perhaps not even the next time, given the *gawat* situation in the country, and the sheer size of the proposed project. He would have to be very diplomatic about the whole thing. He had not really read the proposal. So, on the pretext of discussing it in detail with Desmond Teoh, he went through it paragraph by paragraph.

The proposal entitled "Highway in the Sky," called for the linking up of Cameron Highlands with several other hill resorts in Pahang, Perak and Selangor, the opening up of new areas for housing *en route* s well as the construction of several hotels and a couple of Disney-Land type theme parks. It was presented as a project of mega-proportions that, when completed in approximately twelve years, would generate billions of ringgit in property as well as tourism earnings. The proposal indicated that a Korean partner was willing to come in. On his part Datuk Hang Tuah would have to obtain approval from the respective State and Federal authorities concerned, and more importantly obtain substantial local loans at minimal interest, as well as concessions to collect tolls on the new highways for a period of twenty-five years after completion. Towards the construction and the actual running of the highway project, including the toll collection, several new joint-venture companies would have to be set up.

Desmond Teoh was naturally keen to see some progress on Datuk Hang Tuah's side. The proposal had been with him a good eighteen months; Desmond Teoh and the Datuk had met twice before, the first time in Kuala Lumpur and the second in Taipei. Datuk Hang Tuah was not prepared to confess that, in fact, nothing had been done. Instead he told Desmond that the authorities were interested in the project, and that they had discussed ways and means of raising capital. The land acquisition from the State governments concerned too, would not really be a problem. The answers were vague, but Desmond Teoh seemed to be impressed at what appeared to him to be *some* progress. It was agreed that they would meet again on Monday morning in Datuk Hang Tuah's office. After all it was already Friday afternoon. And they had a full week-end's programme ahead of them. They arranged to meet, at the Datuk's invitation, at a classy Chinese Seafood restaurant at 7.30 p.m.

As the night progressed, following Desmond Teoh's departure, Datuk Hang Tuah knew that by Monday morning he had to come up with some encouraging possibilities for Desmond Teoh regarding the Highway in the Sky project. As he danced in the New Paradise with Sharon, and she warmed up to his embraces, he could not but be convinced that this encounter with Hang Si-To was in fact but an echo of that ancient meeting between Sultan Mahmud Shah and Hang Li-Po; that here were the beginnings of another "conquest of Melaka" by the Chinese. Only this time it was Datuk Hang Tuah and not Sultan Mahmud Shah who was succumbing to silken glamours of Chinese seduction, and the beautiful seducer was not Hang Li- Po, but her reincarnation, Hang Si-To.

Glossary

A: Arabic; H: Hindi; I: Indonesian; M: Malay; P: Persian; S: Sanskrit; T: Tamil; U: Urdu.

Akad Nikah (A)	The Islamic marriage rite
Azan (A)	The Muslim call for prayer
Alhamdulillah (A)	All praise to Allah; also implying Allah be thanked
Angin (M)	Wind; intense desire for something
Angrez log (U/H)	White men, people, particularly the British
Annai (T)	Elder brother
Apsara (S)	Heavenly nymph
Ayat (A)	Verse from the Holy Quran
Baju Kebaya (M)	Tight and short women's blouse worn with a sarung
Baju Kurung (M)	Long and loose women's shirt worn with a sarung
Balai (M)	Audience hall in the palace; any hall
Batik Lepas (I/M)	An unstitched wrap-around skirt of batik material
Batik Sarung (M/I)	A batik wrap-around skirt worn by men or women

Beras kunyit (M/I)	Yellow-stained rice
Beriyani (A/U)	Rice cooked with meat and spices
Berjamu (M)	To feast or the feast itself; in theatre the feast intended for gods or spirits
Berjamu (M)	To feast gods or spirit during or after a ritual performance; also performance involving rituals (persembahan berjamu)
Beta (H/U)	Son
Bhai (U/H)	Brother, also Bhai Saab/Bhai Sahib
Biradari (U/H)	Brotherhood or clan
Bomoh (M/I)	Traditional healer, shaman
Boria (M)	A variety of song and dance from Penang
Burqa (P/U)	Muslim women's outer garment usually black
Chapati (H/U)	Thin, flat bread cooked in a pan
Crore-pati (U/H)	Multi-millionaire
Dalcha (T)	Curry made of beans and vegetables, also with meat
Dupatta (U/H)	Ladies long scarf
Durrie (H/U)	Coarse cotton bedspread or mat
Guru Granth Sahib	Holy book of the Sikhs
Halwai (U/H)	Maker of or dealer in traditional sweets and deserts
Haram (A)	In Islam, haram refers to all things that are forbidden
Haramzadah (U/P)	Illegitimate son; bastard
Hari Raya (M/I)	Festival day; the two major Muslim festivals
Ilmu Dalam (M)	Secret or mystical knowledge of the bomoh

Ilmu Jahat	Same as above, but this time of a negative variety
Ilmu Kebatinan (M)	Same as Ilmu dalam
Imam (A)	In Islam, the leader of a congregational prayer
Insha Allah	God willing
Istana (M)	Palace
Jawan (H/U)	Strong young man, youth
Jiwa Seni (M)	Person sensitive to and fond of the arts
Joget (I/M)	A social dance
Kain Pelikat/Pulaikat (T/M)	Wrap-around skirt for men, of Indian origin
Kalimah Shahadat (A)	In Islam, the affirmation of faith
Kaki Joget (M)	Man fond of the joget dance/dancers
Kanduri/Kenduri (T/M)	Feast
Karma (S)	Fate, Destiny
Kelir (Malay)	Screen in the shadow play to project images of puppets
Khutbah (A)	In Islam, the sermon given as part of congregational prayer
Kismet (P/U)	Fate
Kompang (M)	Frame drums used in ceremonial situations
Kuih (M/I)	Traditional cakes
Kurta (H/U)	Men or women's shirt
Lakh (U/H)	One hundred thousand
Lantai (M)	Landing of a village house
Maghrib (A)	Evening Muslim prayer, the 4th of the day
Maidan (U/H)	Open space
Main puteri (M)	Shaman dance

Mak Cik (M)	Aunty
Mak yong (M)	Traditional dance-theatre form of Kelantan and Patani
Mamak (M)	Termed used in Malaysia to refer to South Indian Muslims
Mandi pelimau (M)	Ritual or ceremonial bath
Mengadap Rebab (M)	In mak yong, the opening dance and song sequence done before the rebab player
Mengkuang (M)	Screwpine
Mentera, Mantra (S)	Invocation text or charm read before performances
Menurun (M)	The descent of a spirit during trance
Minyak angin (M)	Oil used for aches and pains
Mithai (U/H)	Traditional Sweets
Mohalla (U/H)	Section, district, part of a city
Moulvi (U/H)	Islamic religious teacher
Nenek (M)	Grandparent
Nasi beriani	See Beriyani
Nasi dagang (M)	Rice cooked with special herbs in Kelantan
Nasi goreng (I/M)	Fried rice
Nasi minyak (M)	Rice cooked with clarified butter or oil
Niat (A)	Vow of intention to do something
Orang Putih (M)	White man, Westerner
Pagri (U/H)	Turban
Pakora (H/U)	Savoury snack
Pakka (H/U)	Permanent, strong; made of bricks
Pardesi (U/H)	Foreigner; someone not local but from elsewhere
Persembahan (I/M) berjamu (M)	See berjamu above

Pesinden (I)	Female singer in a gamelan orchestra
Pesta (I/M)	Village fair or festival
Pisang goreng (I/M)	Fried bananas; banana fritters
Pooja/Puja (S)	Hindu prayers; also rites in Malay traditional arts
Quran Sharif (U)	The Noble Quran
Sala, Salay (U/H)	Brother(s)-in-law; used as a swear word
Sirih Pinang (M)	Betel leaves and areca nuts
Seth (H/U)	Boss; owner of a business
Sipahi (H/U)	Policeman; soldier
Samosa (H/U)	Sort of Indian curry puff
Sarung (M/I)	Wrap around skirt; also covering; See also Baju kebaya and Baju kurung
Sunnat (A)	In Islam, practices that are considered worth doing
Tarawih (A)	Special evening prayer during the fasting month (Ramadan)
Tawakkal (Ar)	Fate
Teh tarik (M)	Tea which as been mixed by pouring from one container to another
Telekung (M)	Covering worn by women during prayers
Tok Dalang (I/M)	Master puppeteer or story-teller
Tongkat (Malay)	Walking stick
Tosai, Dosa, Masala Tosai (T)	South Indian pancake made of rice flour; at times stuffed with vegetables (masala)
Uppama (T)	Savoury preparation from semolina flour
Ustaz, Ustad (A/U)	Religious teacher
Wayang (I/M)	Puppet, puppet theatre, or performance
Wayang Kulit (I/M)	Shadow play

BIOGRAPHY OF AUTHOR

PROFESSOR DATO' DR GHULAM-SARWAR YOUSOF

Personal Information

Professor Dato' Ghulam Sarwar Yousof graduated in English from the University of Malaya (1964), and did a Doctorate in Asian Theatre at the University of Hawaii (1976). He is one of Malaysia's most distinguished scholars of performing arts and one of the world's leading specialists of traditional Southeast Asian theatre.

He was responsible for setting up Malaysia's first Performing Arts programme at the Science University of Malaysia (USM) in Penang in 1970. Dato' Ghulam Sarwar Yousof served at that university as lecturer and Associate Professor. He joined the Cultural Centre, University of Malaya (UM) as Professor in 2002.

Currently he is Senior Academic Fellow in the Department of English Language and Literature, International Islamic University Malaysia, and also Expert/Pakar at the Cultural Centre, University of Malaya, Kuala Lumpur. He is also Director of The Asian Cultural Heritage Centre Berhad, a private research initiative set up by him to promote research in traditional Asian cultures.

Apart from traditional Asian theatre, his major interests include Asian literatures, folklore studies, as well as South- and Southeast Asian cultures, comparative religion, mythology and, Sufism. In ethnographic and folklore studies he has explored Malay-Indonesian mythology and folk literature, Malay concepts of the soul (*semangat*), and *angin* as well as traditional healing processes, and their role in the cases of disease as well as healing.

As a creative writer, he has published poetry, drama as well as short stories. He has also done a translation of Kalidasa's Sanskrit play *Shakuntala* as well as translations of Urdu poetry into English.

Dato' Ghulam-Sarwar Yousof's most outstanding contribution to academia is in traditional Southeast Asian Theatre. In this area he has carved a unique niche for himself, with meticulous field work and research, in some previously unexplored genres, resulting in the most important existing publication, his *Dictionary of Traditional Southeast Asian Theatre*. His vast collection of fieldwork materials and documentation is currently held by the Asian Cultural Heritage

Centre Berhad. Among other things, he is currently working on a two-volume anthology of Islamic Literature.

Dato' Ghulam-Sarwar Yousof has held visiting positions as professor at several universities, has lectured in many countries in both Asia and Europe on a broad spectrum of culture-related subjects and on altogether unclassifiable disciplines alike to absolute novices and specialized audiences. He has also given readings of his poetry and short stories as well as organised major poetry events in Kuala Lumpur and Penang in conjunction with UNESCO World Poetry Day. He has been, over the decades, involved in various capacities in numerous cultural organizations, national and international, including the Asia-Europe Foundation as Malaysia's official representative and member of the foundation's Board of Governors.

LITERARY PUBLICATIONS

1. **Ghulam-Sarwar Yousof**. *Perfumed Memories*. Singapore: Graham Brash Pte Ltd., 1982. Collection of Poems
2. **Ghulam-Sarwar Yousof**. *Halfway Road, Penang*. Penang. Teks Publishing Company, (1982). Reprinted by The Asian Cultural Heritage Centre, Penang, 2002. (Drama text).
3. **Ghulam-Sarwar Yousof** (comp). *Mirror of a Hundred Hues*. Penang: The Asian Cultural Heritage Centre, 2001. (A Miscellany)
4. **Ghulam-Sarwar Yousof**. *Songs for Shooting Stars: Mystical Verse*. Pittsburgh, PA 15222, USA: Lauriat Press, 2011. (Collection of Poems.)
5. **Ghulam-Sarwar Yousof**. *Transient Moments*. Kuala Lumpur: The Asian Centre, 2012. (Selected Poems)

6. **Ghulam-Sarwar Yousof.** The Trial of Hang Tuah the Great: A Play in Nine Scenes. Singapore: Partridge Publishing, 2014.

7. **Ghulam-Sarwar Yousof** (editor). The Asian Centre Anthology of Malaysian Poetry in English. Singapore: Partridge Publishing, 2014.

Poems in Anthologies

1. Thumboo, Edwin (ed). *The Second Tongue: An Anthology of Poetry from Malaysia and Singapore.* Singapore: Heinemann, 1976.

2. Hashmi, Alamgir (ed). *The Worlds of Muslim Imagination.* Islamabad: Gulmohar, 1986.

3. Malachi, Edwin (ed). *Insight: Malaysian Poems.* Petaling Jaya: Maya Press, 2003.

4. Maya Press. *The Spirit of the Keris.* Petaling Jaya: Maya Press, 2003.

5. Rosli Talif and Noritah Omar (ed). *Petals of Hibiscus: A Representative Anthology of Malaysian Literature in English.* Petaling Jaya: Pearsons Malaysia Sdn Bhd, 2003.

6. Thumboo, Edwin (ed). *& Words: Poems Singapore and Beyond.* Singapore: Ethos Books, 2010.

Random Poems Published

Random poems have appeared in the following journals:

- *Lidra* (Kuala Lumpur)
- *Mele* (Honolulu)
- *Impulse* (Honolulu)

- *Pacific Quarterly* (Hamilton, New Zealand)
- *Dewan Sastera* (Kuala Lumpur)
- *Solidarity* (Manila)

Short Stories

"Lottery Ticket", "Birthday", "Tok Dalang" and "Dewi Ratnasari" in *Mirror of a Hundred Hues: A Miscellany*. Penang: The Asian Centre, 2001.